Archie's®
FAVORITE
Christmas Comics

FAVORITE Christmas Comics

Published by Archie Comic Publications, Inc.
325 Fayette Avenue, Mamaroneck, New York 10543-2318.
www.ArchieComics.com

Printed in U.S.A. First Printing.

ISBN: 978-1-61988-952-1

PUBLISHER/CO-CEO: Jon Goldwater
CO-CEO: Nancy Silberkleit
PRESIDENT: Mike Pellerito
CO-PRESIDENT/EDITOR-IN-CHIEF: Victor Gorelick
CHIEF CREATIVE OFFICER: Roberto Aguirre-Sacasa
SENIOR VICE PRESIDENT,
SALES & BUSINESS DEVELOPMENT: Jim Sokolowski
SENIOR VICE PRESIDENT,
PUBLISHING & OPERATIONS: Harold Buchholz
SENIOR VICE PRESIDENT,
PUBLICITY & MARKETING: Alex Segura
EXECUTIVE DIRECTOR OF EDITORIAL: Paul Kaminski
PRODUCTION MANAGER: Stephen Oswald
PROJECT COORDINATOR/
BOOK DESIGN: Duncan McLachlan
EDITORIAL ASSISTANT/
PROOFREADER: Jamie Lee Rotante
COMPILATION EDITOR: Paul Castiglia

Stories & Art by:

Bob Montana, Dan DeCarlo, Rudy Lapick, Vincent DeCarlo, Harry Sahle, Ed Goggin, Ginger, Frank Doyle, Bob White, Marty Epp, Dan Parent, Rich Koslowski, Barry Grossman, Jack Morelli, Mike Pellowski, Jim Amash, Randy Elliott, Bob Smith, Tim Kennedy, Barbara Slate, Jeff Shultz, Bill Yoshida, Sheldon Brodsky, Al Nickerson, Craig Boldman, Rex Lindsey, Pat Kennedy, Ken Selig, Joe Edwards, Jon D'Agostino, Bill Golliher, Teresa Davidson, Al Milgrom, Fernando Ruiz, George Gladir, Al Hartley, Kathleen Webb, Henry Scarpelli, Alison Flood, Rosario "Tito" Peña, Alex Segura, Gisele, Digikore Studios, Dexter Taylor, Paul Castiglia, Stephanie Vozzo, Vickie Williams, Sal Amendola, Harry Lucey, Greg Crosby

Introductions by: Paul Castiglia

CHRISTMAS IN RIVERDALE!

Introduction by Paul Castiglia

"Deck the halls with warmth and laughter... fa-la-la-la-la-la-la-la!"

Merry Christmas, everyone, and welcome to the first volume in our *Archie's Favorites* series of vintage Archie Comics collections.

In this fun-filled and festive volume, you'll get a taste of what I like to call "An Americana Christmas." And what better friends to serve up such holiday cheer than Archie and his pals? After all, they live in the fabled town of Riverdale... aka "Anytown, USA."

Riverdale is the most welcoming town on earth, where everyone is accepted with kindness and compassion. And you can be sure that a town known for friendship and hilarious fun will definitely get you into the holly jolly spirit when the holidays come around! Even if the Christmas bug hasn't bitten you yet, it won't be too long before Archie, Betty, Jingles, the Sugar Plum Fairy or the others put you in the holiday spirit! After all, many of life's most hysterically funny moments happen during the holidays!

So dear reader, we invite you to read this very special edition—our holiday gift to you! Filled with stories from every decade in Archie's history, this collection covers many holiday themes, with story topics ranging from getting into the Christmas spirit by decorating houses and trees to spreading cheer by giving gifts. There are stories about both dressing up as and actually meeting Santa and his elves (with, of course, special visits from Jingles the Elf and the Sugar Plum Fairy), along with stories about partying with friends by the warmth of the fire and having fun in the winter wonderland outdoors! This book even unearths some of the most unique holiday tales from Archie's history... this collection has it all! We're sure you'll agree it's loaded with both warmth and laughter!

Archie's FAVORITE Christmas Comics

THE EARLY YEARS

Since November, 1941, Archie and his friends have delighted readers both young and old with their hilarious brand of comics entertainment! For nearly as long, they have upheld the traditions of the holiday season. The first Archie Christmas stories appeared in such flagship titles as ARCHIE, JACKPOT, PEP and LAUGH throughout the 1940s. Response to these stories was so great that soon an entire title was devoted to stories of holiday cheer and good will toward all: ARCHIE'S CHRISTMAS STOCKING #1, released in 1954.

ARCHIE ANDREWS' CHRISTMAS STORY
Jackpot Comics #7, 1942
by Bob Montana

THE CASE OF THE MISSING MISTLETOE
Archie #1, 1942
by Bob Montana

CHRISTMAS CHEERS
Pep Comics #46, 1944
by Harry Sahle, Ed Goggin and Ginger

GENEROUS TO A FAULT
Archie Giant Series #5, 1958
by Dan DeCarlo, Rudy Lapick and Vincent DeCarlo

SEASONAL SMOOCH
Archie Giant Series #5, 1958
by Dan DeCarlo, Rudy Lapick
and Vincent DeCarlo

The first-ever Archie Christmas story manages to combine two classic 1940s Archie motifs into one festive tale: a comedy of misunderstandings involving multiple sets of skis intended as Christmas gifts and slapstick action on the ski slopes!

FUNNY NOBODY EVER GIVES ME SKIIS FOR CHRISTMAS ! HMMM..... GUESS THERE'S NO HARM IN JUST LOOKING AT THEM. . . AN' I DON'T NEED THE $4.95 ANYWAY !
IF ARCHIE ONLY KNEW HIS DAD WAS ON THE OTHER SIDE OF THE POST.....
THAT'LL BE $4.95, MR. ANDREWS ! MERRY CHRISTMAS.
MERRY CHRISTMAS !
ARCHIE'LL **NEVER** EXPECT TO GET **SKIIS** HEH I WAS QUITE A SKIIER MYSELF WHEN I WHEN I WAS A LAD !
I KNOW JUST THE PLACE TO HIDE THEM !
NOBODY WILL EVER THINK TO LOOK HERE_ **OMIGOSH, ANOTHER PAIR** !!
GEE, I WOULDN'T WANT TO HURT POP'S FEELINGS. I BETTER GET RID OF MINE. SHUCKS. . . I COULDA SAVED THE 4.95 !
HERE'S A PRESENT, JUGHEAD, OL' PAL _AN' MERRY CHRISTMAS !
???
MEANWHILE ARCHIE'S MOTHER IS RETURNING HOME FROM **HER** SHOPPING !
MY, WON'T ARCHIE BE SURPRISED ! HE'S ALWAYS WANTED SKIIS ! I THINK I'LL KEEP IT AS A SURPRISE _ EVEN FROM FATHER UNTIL CHRISTMAS MORNING !
WOW !
THOSE ARE **SKIIS** IN THERE OR I'LL EAT THE TREE !
2

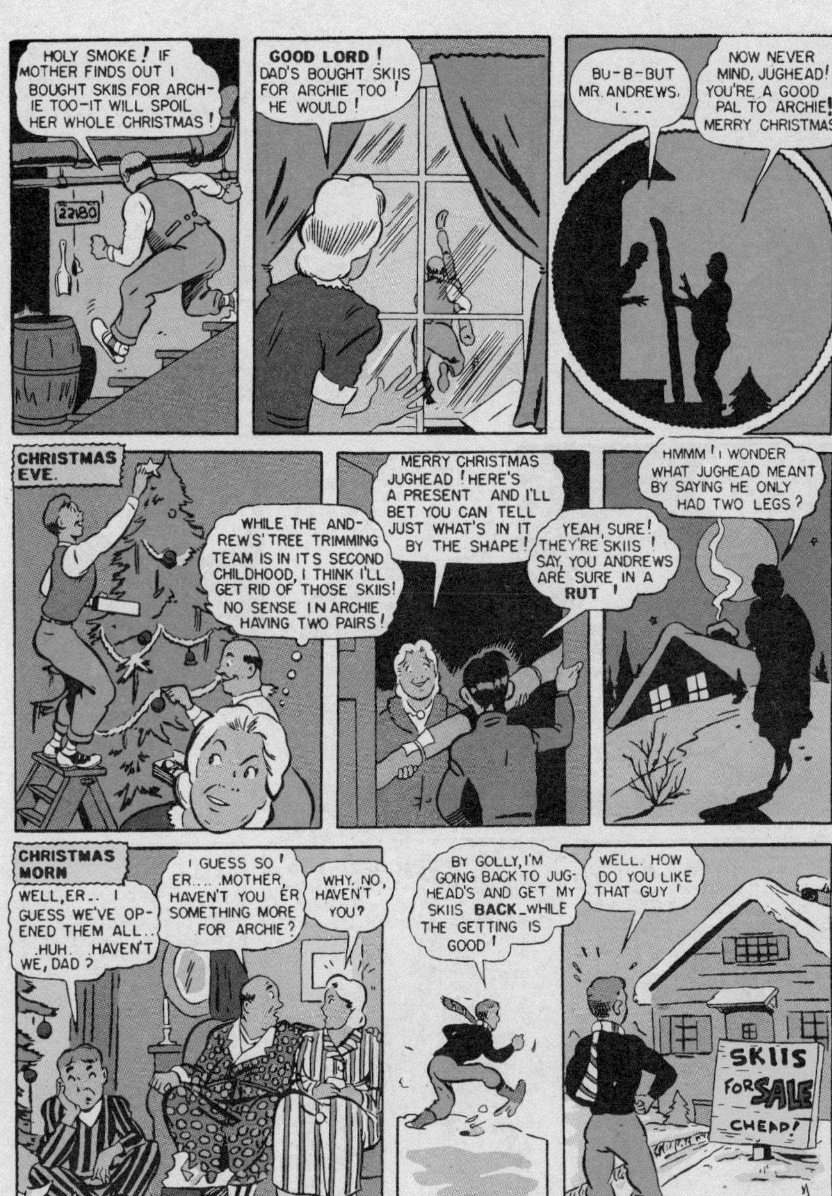
HOLY SMOKE! IF MOTHER FINDS OUT I BOUGHT SKIIS FOR ARCHIE TOO–IT WILL SPOIL HER WHOLE CHRISTMAS!
22180
GOOD LORD! DAD'S BOUGHT SKIIS FOR ARCHIE TOO! HE WOULD!
BU-B-BUT MR. ANDREWS, I...
NOW NEVER MIND, JUGHEAD! YOU'RE A GOOD PAL TO ARCHIE! MERRY CHRISTMAS!
CHRISTMAS EVE.
WHILE THE ANDREWS' TREE TRIMMING TEAM IS IN ITS SECOND CHILDHOOD, I THINK I'LL GET RID OF THOSE SKIIS! NO SENSE IN ARCHIE HAVING TWO PAIRS!
MERRY CHRISTMAS JUGHEAD! HERE'S A PRESENT AND I'LL BET YOU CAN TELL JUST WHAT'S IN IT BY THE SHAPE!
YEAH, SURE! THEY'RE SKIIS! SAY, YOU ANDREWS ARE SURE IN A RUT!
HMMM! I WONDER WHAT JUGHEAD MEANT BY SAYING HE ONLY HAD TWO LEGS?
CHRISTMAS MORN
WELL, ER.. I GUESS WE'VE OPENED THEM ALL.. .HUH. HAVEN'T WE, DAD?
I GUESS SO! ER.... MOTHER, HAVEN'T YOU ER SOMETHING MORE FOR ARCHIE?
WHY, NO, HAVEN'T YOU?
BY GOLLY, I'M GOING BACK TO JUGHEAD'S AND GET MY SKIIS BACK–WHILE THE GETTING IS GOOD!
WELL. HOW DO YOU LIKE THAT GUY!
SKIIS FOR SALE CHEAP!
3

THE NERVE OF THAT GUY CHARGING ME $2.00 TO BUY MY OWN SKIIS BACK!
WHY, LOOK! MOTHER DID GIVE ARCHIE HIS SKIIS!
TEE HEE, YOU SLY OLD RASCAL!
HEH, HEH. YOU'RE A DEVIL MOTHER!
NEXT DAY - ARCHIE CALLS UP VERONICA LODGE...
HELLO, BEAUTIFUL, WHAT'S COOKIN'?

I AM AND READY TO SIZZLE! WHAT'S ON THE FIRE COOKIE?
OH I THOUGHT MAYBE YOU'D LIKE TO HOP A SNOW TRAIN FOR GILFORD, N.H., AND TAKE IN SOME WINTER SPORTS SATURDAY!
OH ARCHIE! I'D JUST LOVE TO! I ADORE NEW HAMPSHIRE IN THE WINTER!

SATURDAY
RIVER
BOY SOME TURN-OUT - HUH VERONICA!

HEY! GET YOUR SKIIS HERE FOR THE SNOW TRAIN!
OMIGOSH! JUGHEAD AGAIN!
SKIIS FOR RENT CHEAP!

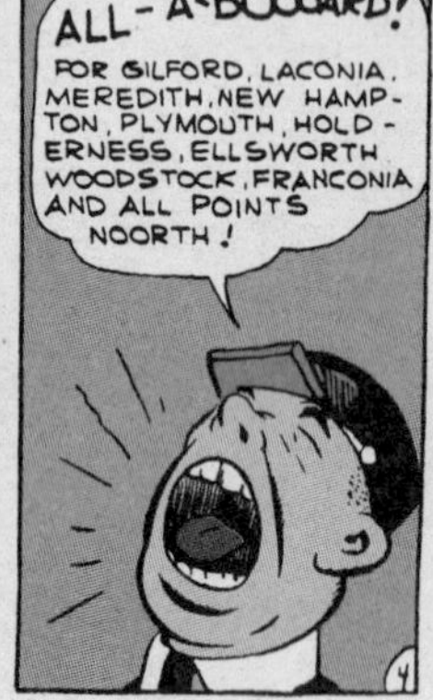
ALL-A-BOOOARD!
FOR GILFORD, LACONIA, MEREDITH, NEW HAMPTON, PLYMOUTH, HOLDERNESS, ELLSWORTH WOODSTOCK, FRANCONIA AND ALL POINTS NOORTH!

ARCHIE, I'LL BET YOU'RE A GOOD SKIIER!
WELL-L --- I DON'T LIKE TO BRAG — BUT I CAN SHOW YOU ANYTHING YOU WANT TO LEARN! NOW F'RINSTANCE — TAKE A CROSS — COUNTRY SLALOMN ..

10 MINUTES LATER...
NOW IN A CHRISTI YOU THROW YOUR WEIGHT ON THE INSIDE SKI AND PUSH OUT WITH THE OTHER, THEN...
I SEE, ARCHIE! DON'T YOU THINK IT'S RATHER CLOSE IN HERE?

WHY DON'T YOU TAKE YOUR JACKET OFF? HERE, I'LL HELP YOU!
ALL RIGHT! THANK YOU!

GULP!
1941 SKI TEAM

ER. AH. D-DID YOU BRING YOUR SKATES, VERONICA?
NO! JUST MY SKIIS!

GILFORD
BELKNAP MOUNTAIN
RECREATION AREA
CENTRE OF TRAMPING
and SKIING
LATCHSTRING ALWAYS OUT

GOSH! ISN'T IT SWELL UP HERE?
JUST PERFECT! I CAN HARDLY WAIT TO GET MY SKIIS ON!

WAHOOO! HERE I COME!

OBOY! AM I HOT!
OOOH, ARCHIE, THAT'S SOLID!
ZIP
5

ARCHIE! ARCHIE! WHERE ARE YOU?
J-J-JUST COOLING OFF!
COME ON, ARCHIE. LET'S GO UP THE CHAIR LIFT AND SKI DOWN MOUNT ROWE!
HUH? UP THERE? I-ER GOSH-UH-WE'VE GOT PLENTY OF TIME FOR THAT!
WELL, I'M GOING UP EVEN IF YOU'RE NOT!
OKAY! OKAY! I'LL HELP YOU ON THE CHAIR!
S'LONG, VERONICA, AN' BE CAREFUL!
HEY! LOOK OUT!
SORRY, BUDDY BUT THAT'S NO PLACE TO STAND!
WHACK!
YOU...YOU... COME BACK AND FIGHT LIKE A MAN!
H-HEY!.. WHAT...?
JEEPERS! I THINK I LEFT MY STOMACH BACK THERE!
6

AT THE TOP...
WHY, ARCHIE! I DIDN'T THINK YOU WERE COMING UP!
NEITHER DID I ... ER ... I MEAN I CHANGED MY MIND SUDDENLY! HEH HEH!
WELL? ARE YOU GOING DOWN, VERONICA?
YOU CAN GO FIRST, ARCHIE! PUT YOUR SKIIS ON!
W-WELL I'M ALL READY I GUESS!
ARCHIE ANDREWS! LOOK AT YOUR SKIIS!
HA! WELL, WHAT A YA KNOW? I'VE GOT 'EM ON BACKWARDS! OH WELL, I'LL JUST TURN AROUND!
BUT NOW YOU'RE POINTING THE WRONG WAY... ARCHIE! ARE YOU STALLING?
HEY! STOP ME! I'M MOVING! I'M SLIPPING!
OoOooOH! STOP HIM, SOMEBODY! HE'S GOING DOWN BACKWARDS!
HALP
SWOOSH
YIIII!!
FIRSH IT WAS LIL' MICE WITH SNOWSHOES H'C NOW ISH LIL MEN SHKIING BACKWARDS H'C I KNEW I SHOULD N'A TOUCHED IT!
7

WELL, WE'RE ALL READY FOR HANS REINMAN'S JUMP!
WHAT IN..?
HOLY CATS! AM I SEEING THINGS OR IS THAT GUY JUMPING BACKWARDS?
WHAT NERVE!
WHAT SKILL!
WHAT A CRASH...
ZING
NOW WE TAKE YOU BACK TO RIVERDALE...THAT'S WHAT THEY DID WITH ARCHIE...
WAUKEWAN
ARCHIE DEAR, JUGHEAD IS HERE TO SEE YOU!. HE'S BEEN WAITING ALL DAY!
H'LO, ARCHIE! THOUGHT MAYBE YOU'D LIKE TO BUY ANOTHER PAIR OF SKIIS ....CHEAP!
IN CASE YOU HAVEN'T HEARD THE NEWS YET— HERE IT IS. HOLD YOUR BREATH! ARCHIE IS IN A MAGAZINE ALL HIS OWN, NOW AND APPEARING IN THE SAME MAGAZINE: "CUBBY," "SQUOIMY, D' WOIM" "JUDGE OWL" AND "BUMBIE THE BEE-TECTIVE" LOOK FOR... ARCHIE COMICS! IT'S SENSATIONAL!

It's double the fun... and double the laughs... when both Archie and Jughead are invited to a Christmas party by identical twins!

GOSH! I COULDN'T REFUSE YOU, ANYWAY--- I MEAN---
ALL RIGHT, ARCHIE. NOW, DON'T BE LATE AND REMEMBER--- YOU'RE TO BE MY BOY FRIEND FOR THE WHOLE EVENING!
JEEPERS, WHAT EYES---WHAT LIPS ---WHAT---- WHAT WAS I DOING BEFORE I BUMPED INTO HER ?
MEANWHILE...
OKAY! I'LL COME TO YOUR PARTY, MISS-- MISS ??
JUST CALL ME JERRY, JUGHEAD!
OKAY, MISS JERRY JUGHEAD -------???
HUH? WE THOUGHT SHE SAID HER NAME WAS JUDY!
JUDY, DEAR, DID YOU GET EVERY-THING FOR OUR PARTY TONIGHT?
YES, AND, OH, JERRY I JUST INVITED THE DARLINGEST BOY!
WHAT'S THIS? ARE WE SEEING DOUBLE? OH,NOW WE GET IT! THEY'RE TWINS!
HIS NAME IS ARCHIE!
THAT'S NOTHING! YOU SHOULD SEE THE HAND-SOME BOY I INVITED! HIS NAME IS JUGHEAD! SO MANLY!
THAT NITE!
I REALLY SHOULD-N'T HAVE SPENT MY LAST BUCK FOR A PRESENT! BUT IT'LL STILL BE CHEAPER THAN TAKING VERONICA OUT!
WELL,WELL! HI YA,JUGHEAD ----AH--SEE YOU LATER!
2
WHAT TH-! SAY, JUGHEAD, ARE YOU FOL-LOWING ME?
WHADDA YA MEAN! SHE INVITED ME, SEE!------ AND FURTHER MORE- I THOUGHT YOU DIN'T LIKE GIRLS!
I DON'T! BUT IT'S A PARTY, AIN'T IT? AN THEY HAVE FOOD AT PARTIES, DON'T THEY?
306

MERRY CHRISTMAS!

JUGHEAD, DEAR! COME IN! COME IN! ---OH--- DELIVERY BOY, TAKE THAT PACKAGE TO THE REAR DOOR!

?
SLAM

WELL, OF ALL THE DIRTY DOUBLE CROSSING LOW DOWN-- -----
ARCHIE! ARCHIE ANDREWS! WHAT ARE YOU DOING OUT THERE? COME IN HERE!

THANKS FOR THE PRESENT, ARCHIE! NOW YOU SIT DOWN IN THE PARLOR AND I'LL BRING YOU SOME ICE CREAM AND CAKE!
GEE, SHE SURE CHANGED QUICK! MUSTA GOT A GOOD LOOK AT JUGHEAD IN THE LIGHT!

OH, ARE YOU GETTING RE-FRESHMENTS TOO, JERRY?
YES, BUT THEY'RE FOR MY BOYFRIEND, JUGHEAD!

GEE, BACK SO SOON!

TAKE YOUR HANDS OFF THAT, YOU HOG!

NOW I'LL SIT RIGHT HERE UNTIL YOU'RE READY FOR SOME MORE, JUGHEAD!

NUTS! I'M GETTING OUT OF HERE! IF SHE CAN'T MAKE UP HER MIND BE-TWEEN JUGHEAD AND ME --SHE'S --IMPOSSIBLE!
IM GOING BACK TO BETTY--- WHERE I'M APPRECIATED!
HELLO!
HERE WE ARE, EVERY-BODY!
WAHOO! HIYA, ARCHIE, YOU JUST GET HERE?
JINGLE BELLS, JINGLE BELLS, JINGLE, JINGLE JINGLE!
ALL RIGHT, YOU CATS! ROLL BACK THE RUGS AN YEZ-DANCE!
HOT DIGGITY! NOW THIS PARTY'S REALLY PERCOLATIN'!
COME ON, SNAKE, ---LET'S CRAWL!
PEST! GO DANCE WITH YOUR OWN GIRL--- ---OH JUG-HEAD!
OOF!
OOPS! WRONG TWIN! POOR ARCHIE!
PHOOEY! I GIVE UP! WHEN WILL I LEARN YOU CAN'T FIGURE WOMEN OUT! I'M GOING IN THE KITCHEN AND EAT MYSELF TO DEATH!
OH THERE YOU ARE, BASHFUL! YOU COULD AT LEAST ASK ME TO DANCE!
4

NOW WAIT A MINUTE! FIRST YOU CALL ME A DELIVERY BOY, THEN A HOG AND NOW BASHFUL! WHAT DID YOU INVITE ME FOR?
BECAUSE I LIKE YOU AND I WANT YOU TO DO ME A FAVOR! NOW COME WITH ME, SILLY BOY!
BOY! IF MY POP COULD ONLY LOSE HIS BAY-WINDOW AS FAST AS I GREW THIS ONE!
TEE HEE! I'VE BEEN SAVING THIS FOR A SURPRISE, WON'T THE KIDS LOVE IT!
WAIT A MINUTE, JUDY! LEMME TAKE A GANDER OF MYSELF IN THAT MIRROR!
GOLLY! I LOOK JUST LIKE OLD SAINT NICK HIMSELF! ... MERRY CHRISTMAS!
HAPPY NEW YEAR!
TWINS! JUGHEAD WHY DIDN'T YOU TELL ME?
I JUST FOUND OUT, TOO.. WHEN I ASKED THE WRONG ONE FOR MORE CAKE!
MERRY CHRISTMAS, GANG!
YEAH! AND THAT GOES DOUBLE!
MERRY CHRISTMAS!
WHAT A CUTE IDEA!
MERRY CHRISTMAS ALL!
HEH, HEH! I'LL BET YOU'RE WONDERING WHERE THE MISSING MISTLETOE IS...HUH..WELL, IT'S MISSING!
DEAR GANG,
EVERY TIME YOU SEND ME A LETTER, I GET INTO MORE TROUBLE. AND EVERY TIME I GET INTO MORE TROUBLE, I GET MORE LETTERS. AND EVERY TIME I GET MORE LETTERS, I GET MORE WORK. FIRST IT WAS PEP COMICS. THEN JACKPOT COMICS. NOW, A COMIC MAGAZINE ALL MY OWN.
BUT I LOVE IT!
AND IF YOU STOP WRITING ME, THE TROUBLE WILL REALLY BEGIN! I WANT TO HEAR FROM EVERY ONE OF YOU, ABOUT MY NEW MAGAZINE. DROP ME A LINE, RIGHT NOW.

It's another Christmas comedy of errors as Archie's gift list inadvertently lands in the hands of the town gossip. Archie can't possibly afford to purchase all the gifts his friends are now expecting!

BUT POP I'VE ALREADY MADE OUT MY LIST!
MAKE OUT ANOTHER ONE... BE PATRIOTIC!
MEANWHILE —
SWISH
WONDER WHAT HAPPENED TO MY OTHER LIST..OH, WELL, I'LL MAKE A NEW ONE ANYWAY.... $31.25 LEFT! LET'S SEE... JUGHEAD A PAIR OF CLAMP-ON SKATES..OSCAR A DOG BLANKET.. AND I'LL JUST GET A SWEATER!!

I CAN'T FIGURE OUT WHAT HAPPENED TO THAT OTHER LIST!!
OH.OH... HERE COMES GABBY--- THE LOCAL RADIO STATION!
YOo.HOo.. ARCHIE!
ARCHIE! WAIT!
SORRY, GABBY, I HAVEN'T TIME.. GOT THINGS T' DO!

BUT, ARCHIE, I FOUND YOUR CHRISTMAS LIST!

YIIPE

LOOK OUT! ARCHIE!
CRASH
BAM

THAT'S MY CAR, YOU YOUNG HOODLUM! THAT'LL COST YOU TEN DOLLARS! NOW!
!?!

SEE WHAT YOU'VE DONE! I HAD TO PAY TEN DOLLARS, ON ACCOUNT OF YOU!
DON'T SHOUT! REMEMBER I STILL HAVE YOUR CHRISTMAS LIST!

HEH, HEH... WOULD YOU CARE FOR A SODA AT TATES, GABBY?
I MOST CERTAINLY WOULD.. LET'S GO!!
INVEST IN WAR BONDS
ALSO WAR STAMPS

WELL! I FEEL BETTER NOW..AND DON'T WORRY ABOUT THAT LIST.. I WON'T TELL A SOUL, HONEST!
THAT'S FINE, GABBY.. I'D BE IN AN AWFUL JAM IF YOU MENTIONED IT TO ANYONE!

HMM..LET ME SEE.. I STILL HAVE $ 20.25...$ 10.00 FOR THE FENDER.. 18.75 FOR A BOND.. AND $ 1.00 ON SODAS.. BUT WORTH IT...
NOW IF I CUT DOWN A LITTLE ON MY GIFTS.. I CAN STILL MAKE IT!

WOW.. ARCHIE WITH GREENBACKS! OR DO MY EYES DECEIVE ME?
SHORTEN SWEET Special 12¢

THIS FIVE DOLLARS WILL JUST SQUARE YOU WITH ME MR. ANDREWS!
ULP! BUT I WAS GONNA PAY YOU MR. TATE.. SOME OTHER TIME!!

$ 15.25! YIPE, I'M GETTIN' RID OF THIS MONEY FAST, WITHOUT EVEN TRYING!
OOH
OWWOO

GABBY! YIPE!!
OHHHH
OHHHH
HOT CHOCOLATE
PICKLES
ICE CREAM
MALTED MILK
ONIONS
CANDY

DOCTOR I. KLIPPEM
TSK.. TSK.. THIS MODERN DEGENERATION!

SHE'LL BE ALL RIGHT, YOUNG MAN, FIVE DOLLARS, PLEASE!
FIVE DOLLARS? GULP!

NOW, I ONLY HAVE $ 10.25.. WOE IS ME WHAT TO DO??

CHRISTMAS EVE....
I HATE SHOWING UP AT THE PARTY WITH THESE MEASLY GIFTS..GULP! GOOD THING THE GANG DON'T KNOW, WHAT I REALLY WAS GONNA BUY 'EM!
LODGE
GOOD EVENING, MAWSTER ANDREWS, AND A VEDDY MEDDY CHRISTMAS!
THE SAME T' YOU, GOGGINS!
WHAT'S HE LOOKIN' UP THERE FOR?
ARCHIE! YOU DARLING!
GEE, BUT YOU'RE WONDERFUL.. AND THIS IS FOR THAT LOVELY NEGLIGEE.. MMM..
?
SO, IT WAS YOU WHO TOLD HER THAT!! YOU, AND YOUR BIG MOUTH! WHO ELSE DID YOU TELL?
G.GOSH, ARCHIE, I ONLY TOLD.. .....
ARCHIE, OH, ARCHIE!
YOU'RE A SWEET, SWEET BOY... MM.. THANKS FOR THE SWEATER SET!....
?
SAY! BLABBER PUSS! WHO ELSE DID YOU TELL?
ARCHIE! HI-YA-PAL!
WELL.. ONLY..

HEY! YOU'RE NOT GONNA KISS ME TOO?!
NAW.. I JUST WANNA THANK YOU FOR THOSE ICE SKATES I HEAR YOU GOT ME!

GATHER 'ROUND KIDS..LET'S OPEN OUR PACKAGES!

NOW TO SEE MY.. OH--- A KERCHIEF!
IMAGINE ARCHIE GETTING ME.. OH....... HANKIES...
HUH? THESE DON'T LOOK LIKE ICE SKATES!

GULP
GULP
GULP

THAT'S NO PLACE FOR ME.. GULP! SNIFF.. SNIFF...

OSCAR, OLE PAL.. I COULDN'T GET YOU THAT NEW DOGHOUSE.. BUT I DID GET THIS BONE!
6

MERRY CHRISTMAS EVERYBODY!!

SAHLE! GINGER

STORY BY GOGGIN SAHLE

"Peace on earth and good will to men" is given an alternative treatment when the boys decide to "give back" to the one among them who has "given until it hurts!"

HOW COME ALL YOU CAN THINK ABOUT IS **FOOD?**
WELL, IT SHOULD BE SOMETHING HE **LIKES!**

AND--ER-AFTER ALL-- *HEH, HEH*- YOU KNOW HOW FOND I AM OF---

JUMPIN' JUPITER!! HE THINKS WE'LL CHOOSE **HIM!!**

I'M TRYING TO BE **MODEST** STUPID!
BUT FACTS ARE **FACTS!**

DON'T CALL **ME** STUPID, YOU EGGHEAD!
OH, YEAH?

HOLD IT, YOU TWO! THIS IS THE SEASON OF GOOD WILL TOWARD MEN!

SURE! SIMMER DOWN, FOR PETE'S SAKE! YOU'RE BEING SELFISH AND NARROW MINDED AND **DISHONEST** AS WELL!

WE **ALL** KNOW WHO DESERVES THE HONOR!
ALL WE HAVE TO DO IS DECIDE HOW TO REWARD ME!

YOU? YOU'VE BEEN GENEROUS?
LIKE A DOG WITH A BONE HE HAS!

I'LL SHOW YOU HOW GENEROUS I AM! I'LL GIVE YOU SOMETHING RIGHT NOW!

COME OFF IT, YOU PEACE LOVING PINHEADS!
DOWN, BOY!

YOU SHOULD BE ASHAMED!! FIGHTING OVER A THING LIKE THIS!

YOU'RE MAKING A MOCKERY OF OUR MARVELOUS IDEA!

SHE'S RIGHT! WE'VE BEEN HEELS!
WE SHOULD LET SOME-ONE ELSE MAKE THE DECISION!

THAT'S RIGHT, WEASEL! WE WERE LOOKING FOR THE FELLOW WHO HAS REALLY LIVED THE SPIRIT OF CHRISTMAS ALL YEAR!
-AND WE NEED YOUR HELP!
WELL, GEE---

--IF YOU MEAN YOU WANT TO KNOW WHAT TO GET ME, I SURE COULD USE A NEW PAIR OF SKATES!

LOOK! WHAT WE WANT IS SOMEONE WHO BELIEVES IN THE OLD SAYINGS!
IT'S BETTER TO **GIVE** THAN RECEIVE!
SURE! THAT'S IT! SOMEONE WHO GIVES, GIVES, GIVES, TILL IT HURTS!
THAT LET'S **US** OUT!
WELL, LET'S GET ALL THE FELLOWS TOGETHER AND DISCUSS IT!
GOOD!
LOOK, BETTY! THE BOYS MUST BE GOING ALONG WITH OUR SUGGESTION!
LET'S EAVESDROP AND SEE WHO THEY PICK!
(GIGGLE!) COME ON!
OKAY, SO **WHO?** **WHO** I SAY, GIVES TILL IT **HURTS?**
HAH!
AND **WHO'S** BEEN DISHING IT OUT ALL YEAR AND NOT RECEIVING ANYTHING IN RETURN?
YEAH! WHO NEEDS TO BE PAID BACK FOR HIS-ER-**GENEROSITY?**
BIG MOOSE!!
-IN UNION THERE IS STRENGTH!
YEAH!

GLEEPS! S-SOME CHRISTMAS SPIRIT!
WE'VE GOT TO WARN MOOSE!
D-UH! WHAT'S THAT?
THE BOYS HAVE ELECTED YOU A SORT OF MAN OF THE YEAR!
M-ME? G-GAWRSH!
THEY PICKED YOU FOR YOUR GENEROSITY!
(SIGH!) AND NOW THEY WANT TO PAY YOU BACK!
D-UH -BUT WHUT'D I GIVE THEM?
INNUMERABLE BLACK EYES, SORE MUSCLES, LOOSE TEETH, BRUISES, SCRAPES AND CONTUSIONS!
-AND NOW THEY'RE GOING TO GET EVEN!
THEY'RE GOING TO GANG UP ON YOU, AND ---
'TIS THE SEASON TO BE JOLLY
FA, LA, LA, LA, LA, -- LA, LA, LA, LA!
PAY HIM BACK TONIGHT BY GOLLY,
FA, LA, LA, LA, LA, ---LA, LA, LA, LA!

DON WE NOW, OUR GAY APPAREL, FALA LA, LALA, LALA LALA! GOT OL' MOOSE OVER A BARREL, FA LA LA LALA, LALA LALA!
STOP! DESIST! HALT!
DISPERSE, YE REBELS!
IS THIS THE SPIRIT OF THE SEASON? IS THIS GOOD WILL TOWARD MEN?
FIE ON YOU!
WHERE'S THAT OL' FORGIVE AND FORGET ROUTINE?
MOBS NEVER SOLVE ANYTHING!
SHE'S RIGHT, BOYS! WE SHOULD BE ASHAMED!
WE'RE A BUNCH OF CREEPS!
SHAKE, MOOSIE! BYGONES ARE BYGONES, MERRY CHRISTMAS!
D-UH! CHEE THANKS, FELLAS!
AND I'M GONNA REVOLVE TUH BE EVEN MORE GENERUS NEXT YEAR THAN I WUZ THIS YEAR!
D-UH! WHUT'D I SAY? WHUT'D I SAY?
THE END

Reggie has found the ultimate loophole regarding his affection for Midge: convinced that Santa won't give him presents if he doesn't "play by the mistletoe rules," Moose begrudgingly allows Reggie to kiss her!

REG! TELL BIG MOOSE ABOUT MISTLETOE!
IT'S JUST A SEASONAL KISSING GAME!

SEE? I KISSED ARCHIE'S GIRL, BUT HE CAN'T OBJECT!
I WOULDN'T DARE!

IF SHE'S UNDER MISTLE TOE SHE'S FAIR GAME FOR ANY FELLOW!
D-UH! I DON'T LIKE THAT GAME!

ANYBODY WHO DOESN'T STICK BY THE RULES HAS TO ANSWER TO YOU KNOW WHO!
(GULP). Y-YOU MEAN...?

YOU WANT AN EMPTY STOCKING CHRISTMAS MORNING?
D-UH! I G-GUESS IT'S NOT SUCH A BAD GAME AT THAT!

NOW YOU'RE GETTING THE RIGHT ATTITUDE!
ER- EXCUSE ME!

D-UH! T-THAT'S MIDGE! H-HE'S KISSIN' MUH GURL, MIDGE!!
SM-MACK!

HOLD IT, PAL! REMEMBER THE RULES!

D-UH! M-MISTLETOE?
DID YOU THINK IT WAS HEDGE LEAVES?

(SIGH) OKAY! I'LL BE A GOOD SPORT!

UNTIL AFTER CHRISTMAS, ANYWAY!
YOU LIVE DANGEROUSLY, CHUM! THAT'S NOT MISTLETOE!

WHAT IS IT?
HEH, HEH! HEDGE LEAVES!

YOU'RE PLAYING WITH FIRE, BUDDY-BOY! I'M WARNING YOU!
YOU CALL THAT, FIRE?

HAH! I HAVEN'T EVEN STARTED TO SMOLDER YET!

CHOK'LIT SHOP

HAVING LUNCH, PAL?
NO STUPID! I'M HITCH HIKING TO HONG KONG!

THEN YOU WON'T MIND IF I BORROW A SPRIG OF PARSLEY!

PUCKER UP, PRINCESS! YOU'RE PERCHED UNDER THAT PLANT AGAIN!

YIKES!! MOOSE!! L-LOOK AT THAT!!
D-UH! IT'S OKAY, JUGHEAD!
SMACK!

SHE'S UNDER THE MISTLETOE!

HOW COME MISTLETOE ON THE MASHED POTATOES?
I COULD HAVE SWORN IT WAS PARSLEY!

SMACK!
SMERP!
S-MACK
SMOOCH

MOOSE, HOW COME YOU LET THAT JERK DO ALL THIS SMOOCHING WITH YOUR GIRL?
D-UH! I AIN'T GOT NO MISTLETOE!

REGGIE SEEMS TO BE DOING ALL RIGHT WITHOUT IT!
WHAT?

HE'S USED PARSLEY, OAK LEAVES, CARROT TOPS AND DANDELION GREENS SO FAR!
D-UH! T-THEY AIN'T MISTLETOE?

SHALL I HOLD YOUR HAT, BUDDY?
D-UH! NO JUGGIE! I CAN'T FIGHT! IT'S TOO CLOSE TUH CHRISTMAS!

I'M TOO FULL OF THE SPIRIT OF LOVE!
WAP!

EVERYBODY'S MUH PAL!
CRACK!

-ESPECIALLY REGGIE!
CRUNCH!

ISN'T THAT RIGHT, PAL?
REGGIE?
SPEAK TUH ME, OLD BUDDY!

TSK, TSK! GIMME A HAND, JUGHEAD! MUH DEAR OLD FRIEND MUSTA TOOK SICK SOMEWHAT!

(GROAN) - LOOK! THE BIG JERK STILL ISN'T WISE! HE SENT ME A WHOLE BOX OF WHAT HE CALLS MISTLETOE!
(GIGGLE) HE'S PRETTY STUPID ALL RIGHT!

WE ALWAYS CALLED THAT STUFF POISON IVY!
THE END

CHRISTMAS TREES AND DECORATIONS

Ah, the Christmas tree! A time-honored holiday tradition. From choosing the tree that's "just right," to cutting it down and bringing it home, to decorating it with all the brightest tinsel, lights and ornaments, a Christmas tree is essential for any family that celebrates the holiday. Peek through a window in Riverdale and you're bound to see a sparkly Christmas tree inside. You're also just as likely to see Archie, Jughead or the rest of the gang getting into one merry mess after another!

A CHRISTMAS TALE
Life with Archie #33, 1965
by Frank Doyle, Bob White and Marty Epp

'TIS THE SEASON FOR EXTREME DECORATING
Betty & Veronica Spectacular #80, 2007
by Dan Parent, Rich Koslowski, Barry Grossman and Jack Morelli

TREE EXPERTS
Veronica #191, 2009
by Mike Pellowski, Dan Parent, Jim Amash, Barry Grossman and Jack Morelli

PRICE CLUBBED
Archie Digest #248, 2008
by Mike Pellowski, Randy Elliott and Bob Smith

The "Christmas spirit" morphs into "competitive spirit" when both Archie and Reggie are determined to chop down the tallest Christmas tree for the town square.

LIFE WITH Archie "A Christmas Tale"

OH, YES I WILL, BETTY!
OH, NO YOU WON'T, RONNIE!
RIVERDALE HIGH GAZETTE
ARCHIE ANDREWS-EDITOR

I HOPE THIS ISN'T A POLITICAL DEBATE... BECAUSE NONE OF US ARE OLD ENOUGH TO VOTE!
JUG!
I'VE BEEN WAITING FOR YOU! I'VE GOT AN IMPORTANT JOB FOR YOU SINCE YOU'RE THE CIRCULATION MANAGER OF THIS NEWSPAPER!
AN IMPORTANT JOB?
YES! I WANT YOU TO HELP ME CUT DOWN A BIG TREE!
RIGHT! AS CIRCULATION MANAGER I PROMISE YOU NOTHING WILL STAND...
WAITAMINIT! IS THIS ANY WAY TO RUN A NEWSPAPER?
OF COURSE! YOU KNOW THAT WE OF THE RIVERDALE HIGH GAZETTE ARE SPONSORING A CHRISTMAS GIFT BENEFIT FOR THE NEEDY CHILDREN OF THIS TOWN!
SO?
SO, MR. WEATHERBEE LET US HAVE THE GYMNASIUM TO SET UP A CHRISTMAS TREE, WHERE THE STUDENTS CAN PUT GIFTS AROUND IT!
SO, WE BUY A CHRISTMAS TREE!
2

ARCHIE WANTS ONE AS TALL AS THE GYM'S CEILING! A TREE THAT BIG WILL COST AT LEAST FIFTY DOLLARS!
OUCH!

THE BIGGER THE TREE... THE MORE GIFTS THE STUDENTS WILL BE ENCOURAGED TO PUT AROUND IT!

ALL RIGHT! BUT WHY DON'T YOU TAKE RONNIE'S OFFER OF FIFTY DOLLARS TO BUY IT?
BECAUSE JUG AND I CAN CUT ONE DOWN IN THE WOODS FOR NOTHING!

I WANT RONNIE TO USE THAT MONEY TO BUY GIFTS FOR THE NEEDY CHILDREN AND PUT THEM UNDER OUR TREE!
OHH, ARCHIEKINS, THAT'S SO NOBLE AND MANLY OF YOU!

THAT'S WHY I PROMISE ALL NEXT MONTH'S DATES TO YOU, ARCHIEKINS!
HOLD ON, GIRL! DON'T FORGET ME!

I CAN CHOP DOWN ANY TREE ARCHIE CAN...AND MORE!
INCLUDING A FEW CHERRY TREES!
3

THAT'S RIGHT! REGGIE IS JUST AS CAPABLE AS ARCHIE!
NEED A TRANSLATOR, MY DEAR? YOU MEAN YOU WANT ARCHIE ALL TO YOURSELF!

OH, NO YOU DON'T, RONNIE!
OH, YES I WILL, BETTY!
OH, NO YOU WON'T, ARCH!
OH, YES I WILL, REG!
RIVERDALE HIGH GAZETTE
205

WAIT! HALT! DESIST! IS THIS ANY WAY TO RUN A NEWSPAPER?

JUGGIE'S RIGHT! WE MUST IRON THIS THING OUT!
I'VE GOT JUST THE SOLUTION!

TO BE FAIR I'LL PROMISE MY DATES TO THE ONE WHO BRINGS BACK THE BIGGEST CHRISTMAS TREE!

WHAT ABOUT THE SECOND TREE?
I'M SURE DADDY WILL BUY IT FOR OUR FRONT WINDOW AT HOME?
4

DO YOU ALWAYS HAVE TO HAVE YOUR WAY?
WAIT, BETTY!

I ACCEPT THE CHALLENGE!
DITTO! AND MAY THE BEST MAN WIN!

WE'RE ALMOST IN THE WOODS, JUG!
I STILL SAY... IS THIS ANY WAY TO RUN A NEWSPAPER?

JUST THINK OF ALL THE NEEDY CHILDREN WHO WILL GET CHRISTMAS GIFTS!

SAY, ARCH, I CAN'T SEE THE FOREST WITH ALL THESE TREES IN THE WAY!

AREN'T YOU AFRAID WE'LL GET LOST?
5

DON'T WORRY, JUG, WE WON'T LOSE OUR WAY! I'VE GOT A TRICK I LEARNED FROM BOY SCOUT DAYS!

YOU USE YOUR HATCHET TO CHOP A SMALL CUT IN A TREE!
CHOP

AT CERTAIN INTERVALS YOU PICK OUT THE LARGEST TREE AND CUT IT!

IT DOESN'T HURT THE TREE! HERE'S ANOTHER ONE!

YOU SEE, BY MARKING A TRAIL YOU WON'T HAVE ANY TROUBLE FINDING YOUR WAY BACK!
CLEVER, THESE BOY SCOUTS!

HEH, HEH!
CHOP!
6

YUK, YUK, YUK!
REGGIE, DON'T LAUGH SO LOUD! ARCHIE AND JUGGIE MIGHT HEAR YOU!
THEY BOTH HAVE EAR MUFFS ON!
YOU'RE DOING A GREAT JOB, BETTY! YOU'VE ERASED ALL SIGNS OF ANY TRACKS!
IT'S EASY BECAUSE THE SNOW IS FRESH!
WHEW! I'M BUSHED! I MUST HAVE MARKED OVER A HUNDRED TREES!
WE MIGHT AS WELL FINISH NOW!
I DON'T MIND GIVING CREDIT WHERE CREDIT IS DUE! THAT CERTAINLY WAS A BEAUTIFUL IDEA OF MINE! YUK, YUK, YUK! I MARKED UP SO MANY TREES ARCHIE AND JUGHEAD WILL NEVER FIND THEIR WAY BACK!
NOW TO FIND OURSELVES A BIG CHRISTMAS TREE!
RIGHT! MR. WEATHERBEE WANTS IT SET UP IN THE GYM BY TONIGHT!
7

HAH! I'VE GOT THIS CONTEST ALL SEWED UP!
RONNIE BETTER KEEP HER PROMISE AND SAVE A MONTH'S DATES FOR YOU!

THEN ARCHIE WILL HAVE TO TURN **ALL** HIS ATTENTION TO ME FOR A **WHOLE MONTH!** (SIGH!)

I WONDER IF THEY WILL EVEN MAKE IT TO SCHOOL TOMORROW MORNING?
WE'LL COME BACK AND GET THEM OUT!

NOW WHERE'S **OUR** TRAIL?
OUR TRAIL?

(GULP!)
OH NO!

YOU AND YOUR **BRILLIANT** SCHEMES! YOU **BELONG** IN HERE WITH YOUR **WOODEN HEAD...BUT I'M LOST!**
NOBODY'S PERFECT, BETTY!
8

THIS IS IT, JUG! IT MUST BE TWENTY FEET HIGH!
IT'S PERFECTLY SHAPED, TOO!

I THINK I'D BETTER STAND OVER HERE SO I WON'T GET HIT BY THE TREE WHEN IT FALLS!

GOLLY! I'M BEGINNING TO GET SCARED!
WE'VE GOT TO GET OUT OF HERE BE-FORE NIGHTFALL!

CCRRRAACK!

THUMP!
AGHHH!

THAT DOES IT! I'M FOR FINDING ARCHIE!
WAIT, BETTY! DON'T LEAVE ME HERE, ALONE!
9

JUG, ARE YOU ALL RIGHT?
(GROAN) IS THIS ANY WAY TO RUN A NEWSPAPER?

YOU REST HERE WHILE I TIE UP THE TREE!
I FEEL LIKE AN ASTRONAUT! THE STARS LOOK SO CLOSE!

THERE! ARE YOU READY TO LEAVE, JUG?
YEAH! I'M HUNGRY!

JUST THINK... FOR A WHOLE MONTH VERONICA WILL BE MINE EXCLUSIVELY!
PHOOEY!

HERE'S ANOTHER MARK, JUGHEAD!

...AND ANOTHER! BOY! WE'LL BE OUT OF HERE IN NO TIME!
GOOD! I'VE NEVER BEEN THIS FAR FROM FOOD!
10

HEY! THIS IS WHERE WE CUT DOWN THIS TREE!
ARE YOU SURE, JUG?

I OUGHT TO KNOW! (GROAN)
THAT MEANS WE WENT AROUND IN A CIRCLE! WE'RE LOST!

LOST? IS THIS...
I KNOW! I KNOW! IS THIS ANY WAY TO RUN A NEWSPAPER!

WELL, DID YOU EVER HEAR OF A CIRCULATION MANAGER WHO IS OUT OF CIRCULATION?
JUST A MINUTE, I SMELL A RAT! IT WOULD BE TO REGGIE'S ADVANTAGE IF HE GOT US LOST... AND I KNOW HE'S IN THESE WOODS RIGHT NOW LOOKING FOR A TREE! YEAH! IT'S HIM ALL RIGHT!

I'M SO HAPPY TO HEAR THAT!
CHEER UP, JUG, I KNOW ANOTHER BOY SCOUT TRICK! C'MON!

YOU SEE, WE'LL FOLLOW THIS RIVER DOWNSTREAM... THEY ALL LEAD SOMEWHERE! IN FACT, I'M SURE THIS ONE GOES UNDER TOOKEY'S BRIDGE, WHERE MY CAR IS PARKED!
11

THE RIVER ICE IS NICE AND FLAT! WE'LL MAKE GOOD TIME GETTING OUT OF HERE!
YEAH! WILL REGGIE BE SURPRISED!

CRACK!

ARCHIE, QUICK! GRAB MY HAND!

HE'S DISAPPEARED! THE CURRENT CARRIED HIM UNDER THE ICE! OMIGOSH! WHAT'LL I DO?

HELP!
THAT'S JUGHEAD!
OVER THIS WAY! HURRY!

JUGHEAD, WHAT'S WRONG?
ARCHIE'S GONE! (SNIFF!) HE'S BEEN UNDER THE ICE FOR FIVE MINUTES!
12

OUCH!

YOU'RE ALWAYS STANDING IN MY WAY, REGGIE!
ARCHIE!

ARCH, HOW COULD YOU STAY UNDER THAT LONG?
MY SCOUTMASTER TOLD ME THERE IS ALWAYS ABOUT AN INCH OF AIR BETWEEN THE WATER AND THE ICE! SO I PRESSED MY NOSE FLAT AGAINST THE ICE AND GOT ENOUGH AIR UNTIL I COULD CHOP OUT A HOLE!

LET'S GET OUT OF HERE BEFORE SOMETHING ELSE HAPPENS!
IT'S ALL YOUR FAULT, REGGIE!

REGGIE ALWAYS WANTED TO BE A BIG WHEEL!
BUT HE GOT THE WRONG END OF THE STICK THIS TIME!
I HOPE WE MAKE IT BEFORE PRESS TIME WITH THIS STORY!
The TALE END

A contest for the "most inspiring holiday display" inevitably inspires Veronica to break out all the bells and whistles!

YOU SIGN UP HERE!
IT'S A CONTEST TO SEE WHO CAN HAVE THE MOST INSPIRING HOLIDAY DISPLAY!
THE WINNER GETS THEIR DISPLAY IN A NATIONAL MAGAZINE AND A CASH PRIZE!
OOH! THIS SOUNDS LIKE FUN!
LET'S SIGN UP, BETTY!
OKAY!
I HAVE A CALL TO MAKE!
SMITHERS, I'LL NEED A MOVING VAN SENT TO THE RIVERDALE MALL!
?
LET'S GO TO "CHRISTMAS WORLD." I CAN GET MY DECORATIONS THERE!
2

56
MAY I HELP YOU?
YES, SEE AISLES 3 AND 4 OVER THERE?
YES.
I'LL TAKE THEM!
HUH?!
I HAVE A TRUCK WAITING AT THE LOADING DOCK!
VERONICA! DON'T YOU THINK YOU'RE GOING A BIT OVERBOARD?!
LOADING DOCK
LITTLE JOHN MOVING
OF COURSE NOT! THIS SHOULD GET ME STARTED!
YOU MEAN YOU'RE GOING TO BUY MORE?!

SOON...
WHO ARE THESE PEOPLE?
THEY'RE MY DECORATING CREW! I'M GOING TO NEED FULL TIME HELP IF I'M GOING TO PULL THIS OFF!
WHAT DOES YOUR FATHER HAVE TO SAY ABOUT ALL THIS?
HE'S AWAY ON A BUSINESS TRIP!
WON'T HE BE SURPRISED WHEN HE GETS BACK!
I'LL SAY!
LET'S TAKE A BREAK AND GO TO YOUR HOUSE!
OKAY!
BETTY! HAVEN'T YOU STARTED PLANNING YOUR DECORATING YET?!
YES! ALL OF MY SUPPLIES ARE RIGHT HERE!
X-MAS STUFF
4

WHAT?! THAT'S IT? BETTY, YOU'RE NOT TAKING THIS VERY SERIOUSLY!
I'M TAKING IT VERY SERIOUSLY!
WHAT ARE YOU PLANNING?
NEVER MIND! YOU'LL HAVE TO WAIT LIKE EVERYONE ELSE!
Hmmm! I WONDER WHAT'S UP HER SLEEVE!
SO...
OUR HOUSES WILL BE GETTING JUDGED 3 DAYS BEFORE CHRISTMAS!
THAT'S TOMORROW!
LET'S GO SEE SOME OF THE HOUSES!
ARCHIE! THAT'S BEAUTIFUL!
IT'S DEDICATED TO MY FAVORITE GIRLS!
5

ONE HALF IS ME... THE OTHER HALF IS YOU!
WAIT ONE MINUTE!!
LOOK AT ALL THESE GIRLS ON THE BACK!
TWO-TIMING US EVEN WITH YOUR HOLIDAY TREE! FOR SHAME!
WOW! JUGHEAD, YOU'VE OUTDONE YOURSELF!
THAT'S NOT SAYING MUCH!
ALL THIS FOOD STAYS NICE AND COLD!
WOULD YOU LIKE A SNACK?
NO!
Oh, WOW! LOOK AT POP'S!
NICE JOB, POP!
HE'LL BE HARD TO BEAT!!
POP'S
POP'S

SPEAKING OF HARD TO BEAT...
WOW! LOOK AT GINGER'S YARD!
I USED ALL SORTS OF COLORED FABRICS!
PLUS DECORATIONS FROM AROUND THE WORLD!
SHE'LL BE HARD TO BEAT, TOO!
RING!
IT'S MY CELL!
IT'S READY! MY YARD IS READY!
ARE YOU READY TO SEE IT?!
SURE!
LET'S GO!
YOU'LL PROBABLY NEED THESE!
SUNGLASSES!?
YOU'LL WANT TO PROTECT YOUR EYES!
7

SOON...
READY... SET...
...LET 'ER RIP!!
FLASH
MERRY CHRISTMAS
OH, MY GOSH!
IS THIS SPECTACULAR OR WHAT?!
8

I'D HATE TO SEE YOUR ELECTRIC BILL!
NOW I WANT TO SEE YOUR DECORATING!
THAT'S IT?!
I MEAN, IT'S CUTE AND ALL...
BUT WHAT MAKES IT SO SPECIAL?
IT RUNS ON ONLY NATURAL ENERGY!
THE LIGHTS ARE SOLAR POWERED!
ALL THE DECORATIONS ARE MADE FROM NATURAL MATERIALS!
EVEN THE GARLAND IS REAL WINTER BLOSSOMS!
IT'S A 100% GREEN CHRISTMAS!
MISS COOPER, WE LOVE YOUR HOLIDAY THEME! WE'RE THE JUDGING COMMITTEE!
THANK YOU!

WELL, WAIT UNTIL YOU SEE MINE! IT'LL BLOW YOU AWAY!
MEANWHILE
I'VE BEEN AWAY FOR SO LONG, IT'LL BE GOOD TO SEE MY FAMILY FOR CHRISTMAS!
ATTENTION, PASSENGERS: DUE TO POOR VISIBILITY, OUR ARRIVAL MAY BE DELAYED!
WE'RE EXPERIENCING MAJOR FOG IN THE RIVERDALE AREA! WE MAY HAVE TO TURN BACK AROUND!
DARN! ALL I WANTED WAS TO GET HOME!
WAIT A MINUTE! SOMETHING IS BREAKING THROUGH THE FOG!!
WOW! THOSE ARE SOME BRIGHT LIGHTS COMING FROM RIVERDALE!!
I DON'T KNOW WHAT IT IS-- BUT IT'S GIVING US ENOUGH LIGHT TO SEE THROUGH THE FOG!
GOOD NEWS! WE'RE CLEARED FOR A LANDING!
10

THANK GOODNESS!
WOW! WHAT'S THAT DOWN THERE?
SOME GARISH HOLIDAY DISPLAY!
HOW TACKY!!
MEANWHILE...
AND THE WINNER OF RIVERDALE'S EXTREME DECORATING CONTEST IS--BETTY COOPER!
BETTY PROVES THAT SOMETIMES LESS IS MORE! HER DISPLAY IS BOLD IN ITS ORIGINALITY!
1ST
WHAT?!
I CAN'T BELIEVE IT! ALL MY WORK FOR NOTHING!
IT'S STILL SPECTACULAR!
1ST
IN FACT, LET'S GO ENJOY YOUR HOUSE!
11

SOON...
HI, EVERY-ONE!
DADDY'S HOME!
VERONICA! ARE YOU RESPONISIBLE FOR THIS OUT-RAGEOUS DISPLAY?!
UH-OH! HERE IT COMES!
I JUST WANT TO SAY IT'S BEAUTIFUL!
IT HELPED ME GET HOME!
I DON'T KNOW WHAT YOU MEAN, BUT I'M NOT ARGUING!
IT LOOKS LIKE BOTH YOUR HOLIDAY DISPLAYS ARE HITS!
YES! ALTHOUGH YOU WON THE BIG PRIZE!
BUT I GUESS I'LL HAVE TO LEARN FROM BETTY!
BECAUSE AFTER WE GET OUR ELECTRIC BILL, I'LL HAVE NO CHOICE BUT TO "GO GREEN"!
END

To avoid the stress of arguments and clashing tastes, the Lodges hire a team of "experts" to decorate their Christmas tree... but they soon learn precision trimming can't beat the joy of togetherness!

SCRIPT: MIKE PELLOWSKI PENCILS: DAN PARENT INKING: JIM AMASH LETTERING: JACK MORELLI COLORING: BARRY GROSSMAN

WE'VE HIRED **PROFESSIONALS** TO TRIM OUR TREE ***FOR US!***

2

IT WAS MY IDEA, ARCHIE. IT'LL SAVE A LOT OF TROUBLE.
WE ALL AGREED THIS WOULD BE A LOT EASIER!
THE EXPERTS DO THE WORK. WE JUST WATCH AND APPRECIATE THE BEAUTY OF THE PROCESS. AND WHEN IT'S ALL OVER, WE HAVE THE PERFECT CHRISTMAS TREE!
SO WHAT DO YOU THINK OF OUR IDEA, ARCHIE?
TRUTHFULLY, SIR, I'M NOT SURE I LIKE IT!
WHAT?!! YOU CAN'T BE SERIOUS! THINK OF ALL THE PROBLEMS THIS ELIMINATES!
THERE'S NO DISCUSSION OR DEBATE OVER WHICH DECORATIONS GO WHERE!
HMMMM... NOW WHICH COLOR BULB GOES HERE?
MOVE THAT ORNA-MENT, DADDYKINS... IT'S TOO CLOSE TO A SIMILAR ONE!
3

NOR DO WE HAVE TO BATTLE TANGLE TROUBLES WITH GARLAND OR STRINGS OF POPCORN!
UGH! THERE'S ANOTHER KNOT IN THIS GARLAND!
ARCHIE! STOP EATING ALL THE POPCORN--!
AND THIS YEAR WE WON'T HAVE TO WORRY ABOUT FAULTY LIGHTS!
GRRR! THIS BULB HAS STOPPED BLINKING!
THIS WHOLE STRAND IS OUT!!
BEST OF ALL, WE DON'T HAVE TO DEAL WITH THE ANNUAL TRAUMA OF PLACING A STAR ON TOP OF THE TREE!
CAREFUL, ARCHIE! CAREFUL!
UH... UHHH...
I CAN'T WATCH!
4

THIS MAY SOUND ODD, BUT I THINK THOSE PROBLEMS MAKE DECORATING A TREE FUN. SO WHAT IF IT'S NOT PERFECT?

EXCUSE ME, MR. LODGE. YOUR TREE IS FINISHED. WHAT DO YOU THINK?
HUH? OH!

IT'S BEAUTIFUL! YOU DID A WONDERFUL JOB!
YES! IT'S ABSOLUTELY PERFECT!
THANK YOU! ENJOY THE HOLIDAYS!

Sigh!
Sigh!
NOW THAT THE TREE IS ALL DONE, I DO SORT OF MISS DOING IT THE OLD-FASHIONED WAY!

YOU KNOW, DEAR, I THINK ARCHIE MAY BE RIGHT ABOUT THIS!
SO DO I. BUT WHAT CAN WE DO ABOUT IT? THE TREE IS ALREADY TRIMMED! WE CAN'T JUST TAKE IT ALL DOWN!
5

WHAT ARE YOU DOING, DADDY-KINS?
I'M ORDERING ANOTHER CHRISTMAS TREE! WE CAN PUT IT IN THE FOYER!

SO YOU MEAN WE'RE GONNA HAVE TWO CHRISTMAS TREES THIS YEAR?!
SURE! WHY NOT? WE'RE RICH, REMEMBER?

LATER...
NOW THIS IS WHAT THE CHRISTMAS SEASON IS ALL ABOUT!
DECORATING A TREE WITH FAMILY AND FRIENDS IS A WONDERFUL HOLIDAY TRADITION!

TA-DAH! THERE! HOW DOES IT LOOK, EVERYONE?
IT'S NOT PERFECT, ARCHIE, BUT AS FAR AS WE'RE CONCERNED, IT LOOKS JUST GREAT!!
END

Nothing can stop Archie's dad's quest to find the perfect... and perfectly priced... Christmas tree!

Archie in "PRICE CLUBBED"

Carl's CHRISTI

HOW ABOUT THIS ONE, POP?

LIKE MOST OF THE TREES WE'VE ALREADY SEEN, IT'S EXPENSIVE, BUT IT *IS* NICELY SHAPED.

SCRIPT: MIKE PELLOWSKI
PENCILS: RANDY ELLIOTT
INKS: BOB SMITH

TAKE IT FROM ME... THIS TREE WILL BE MOSTLY BALD BY NEW YEARS' DAY.
WHEN IT COMES TO BALDNESS, POP IS AN EXPERT!

AH-HUM!
HEH! HEH! EXCUSE ME, POP! I DIDN'T MEAN IT THE WAY IT SOUNDED!

WE'VE ALREADY BEEN TO THREE PLACES, FRED.
WHEN ARE YOU GOING TO DECIDE ON A TREE?
I'M SORRY, MARY, BUT WHEN IT COMES TO A CHRISTMAS TREE, I WANT THE FRESHEST ONE I CAN GET.
EXIT

THE HIGH COST OF CHRISTMAS TREES THIS YEAR IS BAD ENOUGH. I WILL NOT SETTLE FOR A DRIED OUT TREE.
$35&UP

EXCUSE ME, NEIGHBOR... I KNOW WHERE YOU CAN GET THE FRESHEST TREE AROUND AT A GREAT PRICE!
HUH! WHERE?
2

THERE'S A "CUT YOUR OWN" CHRISTMAS TREE FARM OUT ON ROUTE 182. IT'S CALLED "SANTA CLAUS ACRES."
REALLY? AND YOU SAY THE PRICES ARE LOW?
Carl's CHRISTMAST
THEY'RE THE BEST AROUND. THE MONEY THEY SAVE ON LABOR AND SHIPPING THEY PASS ON TO THE CONSUMER.
WOW! THANKS FOR THE TIP, PAL.
SO WHAT DO WE DO NOW, POP... TRY ANOTHER PLACE?
NO! TOMORROW WE DRIVE OUT TO SANTA CLAUS ACRES TO CUT DOWN OUR OWN CHRISTMAS TREE.
THE NEXT MORNING...
COULDN'T WE HAVE LEFT LATER AND TAKEN THE TIME TO HAVE A GOOD BREAKFAST, FRED?
NO, MARY, I WANT TO GET AN EARLY START. THIS PLACE WILL TAKE A WHILE TO GET TO.
3

GULP! JUST HOW FAR AWAY IS THIS PLACE, POP?
DON'T WORRY ABOUT THAT, ARCHIE. WE'LL HAVE A NICE, RELAXING DRIVE IN THE COUNTRY.

MANY, MANY MILES LATER...
ARE WE EVER GOING TO GET THERE, POP?
WE WON'T IF I DON'T STOP FOR GAS! I'M ALMOST EMPTY.
GAS&GO
GAS &

I'LL PUMP THE GAS, POP.
THANKS, SON. I WANT TO STAY IN A CHEERFUL MOOD, AND LOOKING AT THE PRICE OF A GALLON OF GAS TENDS TO DEPRESS ME.

OKAY, POP. WE'RE GOOD TO GO.
THANK GOODNESS. THIS FILL-UP WILL JUST ABOUT EMPTY MY WALLET OF CASH.

LUCKILY, THERE'S AN ATM OVER BY THAT DINER.
WHILE WE'RE HERE, CAN WE GRAB A BITE TO EAT? I'M STARVED.
COUNTRY KITCHEN DINER
ATM
N DINER

HOW ABOUT IT, FRED? AFTER ALL, WE DID SKIP BREAKFAST!
WELL... OKAY. COME ON. LET'S EAT.
4

LATER...
YUM! THANKS FOR THE PANCAKES, POP. THEY SURE HIT THE SPOT.
I'M GLAD YOU ENJOYED THEM... BUT YOU ATE LIKE YOU'VE BEEN TAKING LESSONS FROM JUGHEAD!
COUNTRY KITCHEN
OPEN
ATM

THAT LITTLE REST STOP COST ME A PRETTY PENNY.
DON'T WORRY, POP. JUST THINK OF ALL THE MONEY YOU'LL SAVE ON OUR TREE.
GAS

FURTHER DOWN THE ROAD...
HO! HO! HO!
SANTA CLAUS ACRES
CHRISTMAS TREES
DRIVE-IN
THANK GOODNESS! HERE WE ARE AT LAST.

PICK OUT THE TREE YOU WANT, CUT IT DOWN, AND DRAG IT BACK HERE.
RIGHT. LET'S GO, FAMILY!
WE'RE RIGHT BEHIND YOU, POP.

WOW! LOOK AT THAT TREE! I THINK IT'S PERFECT!
IS THIS ONE FRESH ENOUGH, FOR YOU, POP?
HA! HA! IT SURE IS!
5

ATER THE TREE IS CUT...
THANKS AGAIN. IT'S BEEN A PLEASURE DOING BUSINESS WITH YOU. YOUR TREES ARE A REAL BARGAIN.
YOU'RE WELCOME. HO! HO! HO! HAPPY HOLIDAYS!

NOW THAT WE'VE GOT OUR TREE, LET'S GET IT HOME AND DECORATE IT.

LATER, AT THE ANDREWS HOUSE...
ADMIT IT, MARY...WE GOT A TERRIFIC TREE THIS YEAR. IT'S TOTALLY FRESH, AND IT WAS VERY AFFORDABLE.

I LOVE THE TREE, FRED, BUT IT ENDED UP COSTING US MORE THAN ONE FROM A LOT. JUST CONSIDER HOW MUCH WE SPENT ON THE TRIP ALONE.
THAT'S TRUE, MARY.

BUT THE COST OF ENJOYING A BEAUTIFUL CHRISTMAS TRADITION TOGETHER WITH ONE'S FAMILY IS... PRICELESS!
I AGREE, POP, AND PLUS...THERE'S NOT A SINGLE PINE NEEDLE ON THE FLOOR!
THE END

Betty and Veronica in
"SNOW FLAKES"
SOMEONE IS MAKING SNOWMEN TO RESEMBLE *REAL* PEOPLE!
HA! HA! THAT'S JUGGIE ALL RIGHT!

HILARIOUS!
EMPTY WALLET

HA! HA! WAIT TILL THE BEE SEES THIS!
MOUNT BALDY

THAT'S NOT FUNNY!
MISS "I SHOP TILL I DROP"
END

Archie's FAVORITE Christmas Comics

GIFTS & GIVING

The holiday season is the season of giving, and the best Archie Christmas stories have always reflected that spirit in a myriad of ways. This selection of tales presents it all—from the heartwarming to the humorous and everything in-between!

HOLIDAY RUSH
Holiday Fun Digest #11, 2006
by Mike Pellowski, Tim Kennedy, Rich Koslowski, Barry Grossman and Jack Morelli

GIFT EXCHANGE
Betty & Veronica #87, 1963
by Frank Doyle, Dan DeCarlo and Vincent Decarlo

CHRISTMAS MISGIVINGS
Veronica #60, 1997
by Barbara Slate, Jeff Shultz, Rudy Lapick, Barry Grossman and Bill Yoshida

STAMP OF APPROVAL
Archie Giant Series #6, 1959
by Frank Doyle, Dan DeCarlo, Rudy Lapick, Sheldon Brodsky and Vincent DeCarlo

GIFT EXCHANGE
Holiday Fun Digest #11, 2006
by Mike Pellowski, Tim Kennedy and Al Nickerson

SNUGGLE UP
Betty & Veronica #244, 2009
by Dan Parent, Jeff Shultz, Rich Koslowski, Barry Grossman and Jack Morelli

FIT TO BE YULETIDE
Jughead #125, 2000
by Craig Boldman, Rex Lindsey, Rich Koslowski, Barry Grossman and Bill Yoshida

THE GIFT HORSE LAUGHS
Archie Digest #248, 2008
by Mike Pellowski, Pat Kennedy and Ken Selig

Betty & Veronica lament the fact that the stores rush the holidays months before they actually hit... until Mr. Lodge gives them some early Christmas gifts!

Sigh!
WHAT'S WRONG, BETTY? AREN'T YOU LOOKING FORWARD TO HAVING LUNCH DOWNTOWN WITH ME AND DADDYKINS?
SEASONS GREETINGS

SCRIPT: MIKE PELLOWSKI PENCILS: TIM KENNEDY INKS: RICH KOSLOWSKI
COLORS: BARRY GROSSMAN LETTERS: JACK MORELLI

IT SEEMS LIKE RETAILERS TRY TO USHER IN THE HOLIDAY SEASON EARLIER AND EARLIER EACH YEAR!
HAPPY HOLIDAY
BIG 'n' TALL
VIC'S VIDE
HUGE PRE-PRE-CHRISTMAS SALE
HOLID DVD SALE
WHAT THEY WANT TO USHER IN IS THE HOLIDAY *SHOPPING* SEASON, BETTY!

AS SOON AS IT'S SO LONG TO THANKSGIVING, THE STORES GET READY TO SAY *BUY! BUY!* TO CHRISTMAS!
AFTER YOU FINISH DECORATING THE STOREFRONT, COME INSIDE AND PUT OUR NEWEST GIFT ITEMS IN THE WINDOW!
2

THE NEXT THING YOU KNOW, SANTA CLAUS WILL COME STROLLING PAST!
TEE-HEE! I DOUBT THAT, BETTY!

OOPS! I GUESS YOU SPOKE TOO SOON!
THAT'S FOR SURE!

HO! HO! HO! HAPPY HOLIDAYS, LADIES! VISIT ME INSIDE 'ELMER'S' FOR THE BEST PRE-CHRISTMAS BARGAINS AROUND!
SALE
ELECTRON
SORRY, SANTA! SOME OTHER TIME! WE HAVE A LUNCH DATE!

SOME STORES WILL DO ANYTHING TO PUT SHOPPERS IN THE RIGHT MOOD TO SPEND MONEY!
DING DING
SHOP at SAL'S SHOES
3

I GUESS YOU CAN'T BLAME THE STORES! THEY ARE IN BUSINESS TO EARN PROFITS!
AND CHRIST-MAS IS THEIR BUSIEST SEASON!
PLUS, THE DECORATIONS ARE PRETTY TO LOOK AT!
LOOK! HERE'S DADDYKINS NOW!
HELLO, GIRLS! YOU'RE RIGHT ON TIME!
HAPPY HOLIDA
SURPRISE!
GOSH, DADDYKINS! WHAT'S THIS?!
GEE! THANK YOU, MR. LODGE!!
4

IT'S NOTHING MUCH! LET'S JUST SAY THEY'RE VERY EARLY CHRISTMAS PRESENTS!

SEEING ALL THE STORE DECORATIONS PUT ME IN A JOLLY MOOD FOR GIVING, SO... HAPPY HOLIDAYS!

THANK YOU SO MUCH, DADDYKINS! WE'LL OPEN THEM AT LUNCH!
THIS WAS VERY GENEROUS OF YOU!!
YOU'RE BOTH VERY WELCOME! AFTER ALL, CHRISTMAS WILL BE HERE BEFORE YOU KNOW IT!

HO! HO! HO! NOW LET'S GO HAVE LUNCH! I RESERVED A TABLE FOR US!
WELL, BETTY, I GUESS THERE'S NOTHING WRONG WITH A LITTLE CHRISTMAS CHEER -- NO MATTER WHAT TIME OF YEAR IT HAPPENS TO BE!!
The END

Veronica is feeling extra generous this holiday season. So much so that she's gifted Reggie to Betty!

Betty and Veronica in 'GIFT EXCHANGE'

BETTY, DARLING, AS MY DEAREST, MOST LIFELONG, VERY CLOSEST FRIEND, I WANT TO BESTOW UPON YOU MY MOST CHERISHED POSSESSION!

GOLLEE!

WHAT ABOUT ARCHIE ?
OH, **HE'S** OKAY!

-BUT REGGIE IS MY **REAL** LOVE!
MAN! **THAT'S** BEEN A CLOSELY GUARDED SECRET!

GREATER LOVE HAS NO GIRL, ...

... THAN THAT SHE'D GIVE UP HER TRUE LOVE TO HER FRIEND!
?
?

GO QUICKLY, MY DARLING!

DON'T HESITATE! TAKE HIM AND GO! I FEEL MYSELF WEAKENING ALREADY!
SOB

SLAM!
?
2

SHE'S A GREAT GIRL, BUT SHE'S GOT AS MUCH ACTING ABILITY AS A WOODEN BAT!

SHE GOT RID OF BOTH OF US WITH-OUT A FIGHT, THOUGH!
YOU THINK WE CRAMP HER STYLE?

WELL, YOU'RE AFTER **HER** AND I'M AFTER **ARCHIE**!

NOW SHE'S FREE OF BOTH OF US!

-AND SHE MADE IT SEEM LIKE A **FAVOR** TO US!

...SO WE CAN'T OBJECT!
I CAN! SHE'S ENTIRELY **TOO** GENEROUS!

Y-EAH!
SOMEHOW, SHE OUGHT TO GET PAID BACK FOR BEING SO NICE!
3

D-UH! HI, YOU TWO!
MOOSE!

MOOSIE! LOOK WHAT MY BIG, WONDERFUL, GENEROUS FRIEND RONNIE GAVE ME!
I DON'T SEE NOTHIN'!

REGGIE! SHE GAVE ME REGGIE!

D-UH! SHE'S MAD ATCHA?

NOT AT ALL! IT WAS A GESTURE OF FRIENDSHIP!

I NEVER HEARD OF NOBODY GIVIN' AWAY PEOPLE BEFORE!

WELL, YOU KNOW HOW RONNIE IS!
SHE LIKES TO START FADS!
4

WOULDN'T IT BE NICE IF I HAD SOMEONE TO GIVE TO RONNIE?

I FEEL I OWE HER SOMETHING!
OH, YOU DO! YOU DO!

SAY! HOW ABOUT MOOSE?
?

D-UH! ME? YUH WANTA GIVE ME TUH VERONICA?

NO! HE HAS A GIRL!
MIDGE!

NO I DON'T! MIDGE IS VISITIN' HER AUNT FER A WHOLE WEEK!
W-ELL, IF YOU'D LIKE TO BE MY GIFT TO RONNIE...

GAWRSH! HURRY UP AN' GET ME GIFT-WRAPPED!!
5

YOU SHOULD HAVE SEEN THEIR FACES AS I PUSHED THEM OUT THE DOOR!
BONG! BONG!
ULP! MOOSE!!
?
D-UH! READ THE TAG!
YOU'RE... YOU'RE A GIFT FROM BETTY?
I'M ALL YOURS!
HEY? HOW ABOUT ME?
D-UH! YEAH! HOW ABOUT THAT?
WHUT ARE YOU DOIN' HERE WITH MY GURL?
ONE GOOD TURN DESERVES ANOTHER!
YOU'RE ALL HEART, BETTY!
The End

The gang think they've figured out what Veronica's giving them for Christmas—until they find out they're spying in the wrong shopping bag!

HI, EVERYBODY! I JUST FINISHED MY CHRISTMAS SHOPPING!
POP'S

I CAN'T WAIT 'TIL YOU SEE EVERYTHING I...

... BOUGHT!
UH-OH!

I FORGOT TO CALL DADDY!

I'D BETTER TELL HIM I'LL BE HOME FOR DINNER!
POP'S
2

AND DON'T LOOK INTO MY BAGS!
SUNDAE 5¢
ALL THOSE PRESENTS ARE A BIG SURPRISE!
EAR-MUFFS!
A SWEATER!
ICE SKATES!
3

HOW THOUGHTFUL OF RONNIE TO REMEMBER MY RIPPED SKATES FROM LAST YEAR!

ONLY MY BEST FRIEND IN THE WHOLE WORLD WOULD KNOW MY FAVORITE PINK!

HOW SWEET OF RONNIE TO REMEMBER I HAD A COLD ALL WINTER!
ACHOO!

I HAVE TO HURRY! DADDY IS EXPECTING ME!

WE'LL SEE YOU AT THE LAKE!
BYE, RONNIE!
BYE!

AFTER WHAT RONNIE BOUGHT ME, I CAN'T JUST GIVE HER A SILLY STUFFED SANTA CLAUS!

4

THAT BOX OF STATIONERY FOR RONNIE DOESN'T COMPARE TO MY BEAUTIFUL SWEATER!

MAYBE I SHOULD BUY VERONICA ANOTHER CHOCOLATE REINDEER!

AND SOON...
SHE DESERVES SOMETHING EXTRA SPECIAL!
CANDY CORNER
SALLY'S
SECRE

THAT NIGHT...
GREAT SPIN, BETTY!

LOOK, MOMMY! HOW CAN I TWIRL LIKE THAT?
PRACTICE, PRACTICE, PRACTICE!
LOOK, EVERYBODY!
5

HERE I COME!

SHE HAS ON MY ICE SKATES!
THAT'S MY SWEATER!
WHY IS SHE WEARING MY EARMUFFS?

ISN'T MY OUTFIT AWESOME?!

I WANTED TO SURPRISE ALL OF YOU!
YOU SURE SURPRISED ME, RON!
ME TOO!
ME THREE!
END

Betty is on a green stamp collecting binge, hoping to trade them all in for a worthy premium. Naturally, Veronica scoffs at the idea... until she sees the handsome young man Betty meets in her quest!

OH, COME OFF IT, NOW!
SO HELP ME, LAMBIE-PIE! THAT'S WHAT SHE WANTS!

HIS MOTHER JUST THROWS THEM AWAY! I ONLY WANT HIM TO SAVE THEM FOR **ME**!
THOSE STAMPS YOU GET WITH YOUR **GROCERIES**?

YOU CAN GET WONDERFUL PREMIUMS WITH THEM!
PREMIUM BOOK
GREEN STAMPS

BUT WHO WANTS TO GO TO ALL THAT **BOTHER**?
I DO!

HEE, HEE! WHY DON'T YOU GO OVER TO **MY** HOUSE?

OUR HOUSE KEEPER BUYS FOOD LIKE IT'S GOING OUT OF STYLE!

WHERE'D SHE GO?
ZOOM!

HELLO, BETTY! I'VE JUST FINISHED MY SHOPPING FOR THE LODGE'S!
DO YOU SAVE GREEN STAMPS?

HEAVENS, NO! DO YOU WANT THESE?
G-GOLLY! THANKS! WHAT A HAUL!

NOW THAT'S WHAT I CALL AN ECONOMY MINDED GIRL!

"GREEN STAMPS?" NO KIDDING?
ISN'T THAT SILLY?

HERE COMES OUR STICKY TONGUE ODD-BALL NOW!

THIS IS A STICK-UP, GIRLIE! YOUR MONEY OR YOUR LIFE!
TAKE THEM BOTH IF YOU WANT!

--BUT, PLEASE, SIR! DON'T TAKE MY GREEN STAMPS!
YUK! YUK!

HMPH! FUNNY, FUNNY, FUNNY!

YOU'LL ALL STOP LAUGHING WHEN YOU SEE THE BEAUTIFUL PREMIUM I TRADE THESE STAMPS FOR!
PREMIUM BOOK
GREEN STAMPS

TOASTER, NECKLACE, HAIR DRYER, TENNIS RACK---
WAH! I BWOKE MY WIDDLE SLED!

OH, YOU POOR KID! THAT'S AWF---
DR

-- SAY! DON'T GO AWAY!
I'M GOING TO GET YOU A **BRAND NEW SLED!**
PREMIUM BOOK
GREEN

THERE WE ARE! HOW WOULD YOU LIKE **THAT** ONE?
OH, BOY!

POOR LITTLE TOT!
-AND WHO NEEDS A HAIR DRYER ANYWAY!
PREMIUM REDEMPTION CENTER
GREEN STAMPS

THERE YOU ARE, MISS!
THANK YOU!

HE'LL LOVE IT! HE'LL JUST LOVE IT!

I CAN'T WAIT TO SEE HIS FACE, WHEN I---

WHAM!

YOU CLUMSY OX! IF YOU BROKE MY SLED, I'LL---
THAT'S A MIGHTY STRONG LITTLE SLED YOU'VE GOT THERE, MISS!

(GROAN) I WISH I COULD SAY THE SAME FOR MY ANKLE!
OH, YOU POOR BOY! Y-YOU SPRAINED IT!

C-CAN YOU WALK ON IT?
OUCH! I'M AFRAID NOT!

CHEE, THANKS! THIS IS FINE!
YOU'LL BE HOME IN A JIFFY!

TSK! THAT IDIOT! WASTING HER TIME WITH THOSE SILLY STAMPS!

OBVIOUSLY SHE DOESN'T THINK IT'S WASTED!
LOOK!

(GULP!) G-GREEN STAMPS?
OF COURSE!

VERONICA! YOU BLIND, BLIND FOOL!
SHE WANTS A SLEIGH?
YOK! SHE THINKS HE'S THE PREMIUM!
?

M-MISS VERONICA! WHAT WILL I DO WITH ALL THIS FOOD!
FOOD- SCHMOOD! JUST GET THOSE GREEN STAMPS!
FOOD SHOP
AL'S GRO
DELI
GROCERY
THE END

Chuck and Moose are having a hard time figuring out what to get their girlfriends for Christmas, until they make suggestions for each others' girls!

CHUCK and® MOOSE IN GIFT EXCHANGE!

RIVERDALE MALL INFORMATION

HEY, MOOSE! WHAT ARE YOU DOING HERE?

I'M SHOPPING FOR A CHRISTMAS PRESENT FOR MIDGE. WHAT ARE YOU UP TO?

PELLOWSKI

KENNEDY

nickerson

HUMM...NANCY IS THINKING OF STARTING A FITNESS PROGRAM. PERHAPS SHE'D LIKE A NICE SPORT CARRY-ALL BAG.

NAH! NANCY REALLY ISN'T THAT MUCH OF A SPORTS TYPE!
UGH! OOF!

NANCY LIKES JEWELRY! EARRINGS ARE A POSSIBILITY OR HOW ABOUT A BOOK?
NOVEL APPROACH
Books • Magazines

PERFUME? CDs? GLOVES? GULP! WHICH GIFT IS THE RIGHT GIFT!?! I JUST DON'T KNOW!

MEANWHILE...
HEY! MAYBE MIDGE WOULD LIKE A FANCY PURSE!
PURSE
Sale

NO WAY! MIDGE IS MORE INTO SPORTS GEAR!
?
JOGGING TRAIL
2

BUT MAYBE I SHOULD BUY HER A TENNIS BRACELET OR A NICE WATCH.
JACK'S
JEWELRY
SHOE
WOR

LATER...
ARRUGH! I DON'T KNOW WHAT TO DO! I'VE BEEN TO DOZENS OF STORES, AND I HAVEN'T SEEN ANYTHING THAT I REALLY LIKE!

HEY, MOOSE! WE MEET AGAIN. HOW ARE YOU MAKING OUT?
AWFUL, CHUCK! HOW ABOUT YOU?

I'M BATTING ZERO. MAYBE WE SHOULD PUT OUR HEADS TOGETHER ON THIS.
I'M WILLING TO TRY ANYTHING. HAVE YOU SEEN ANYTHING OF INTEREST?

WELL...I DID CONSIDER GETTING A NICE SPORTS CARRY-ALL FOR NANCY. HOW WAS YOUR LUCK?
I SAW A FANCY PURSE I THOUGHT ABOUT BUYING.
3

HEY! I THINK A PURSE MIGHT BE PERFECT FOR NANCY.

A NEW SPORTS CARRY-ALL WOULD MAKE A GOOD GIFT FOR MIDGE. HER OLD ONE IS KIND OF RATTY.

PUTTING OUR HEADS TOGETHER REALLY WORKED.

IT SURE DID, PAL. NOW LET'S GO GET THOSE GIFTS!

SINCE WE'RE BUYING THE GIRLS PRESENTS TOGETHER, LET'S ALSO GIVE THEM THEIR GIFTS AT THE SAME TIME.

GOOD IDEA! WE CAN MEET AT MY HOUSE OVER THE HOLIDAYS. IT'LL BE FUN!

DURING THE HOLIDAYS AT MOOSE'S HOUSE...

THIS PURSE IS GOING TO BE THE PERFECT PRESENT.

I JUST KNOW MIDGE IS GOING TO LOVE THIS SPORTS CARRY-ALL BAG.

DUH... UH-OH!
GULP! IT SOUNDS LIKE WE GOOFED!
HMMM... MAYBE NOT. DOES YOUR PACKAGE HAVE A LABEL ON IT?
NO. WHY?
NEITHER DOES MINE! LET'S SWITCH!
HEY! OKAY!
WE'RE BACK, GIRLS! HAPPY HOLIDAYS! OPEN THESE!
WOW! THANK YOU, GUYS! AFTER WE OPEN THOSE, WE'LL GIVE YOU YOUR GIFTS.
MINUTES LATER...
OH, CHUCK! THIS SPORTS CARRY-ALL IS A TERRIFIC GIFT! I'LL GET GREAT USE OUT OF IT!
WHEW!
WHEW!
I JUST LOVE THIS PURSE, MOOSE! IT'S PERFECT!
END

Seeking ideas that will save some money this holiday, the gang decide to do a "Secret Santa" giveaway... but once they see their presents they'll wish the idea had stayed a secret!

Betty and Veronica® in SNUGGLE UP!

IT WAS A GOOD IDEA TO DO A "*SECRET SANTA*" GET TO-GETHER HERE AT POP'S!

THAT WAY WE ONLY HAVE TO SPEND MONEY ON *ONE* PRESENT... BUT EVERYONE GETS SOMETHING!

WOW! A CREPE MAKER!
I GUESS I'LL HAVE TO BRANCH OUT INTO FRENCH CUISINE!

LET ME GUESS WHO PICKED MY NAME...
BETTY?

YOU GOT IT!
THIS SEEMED LIKE A "BETTY" TYPE OF PRESENT!

AND AS THE DAY GOES ON...
COOL! A NEW CD BY MUSTACHE CONTORTION!

A POP TATE'S GIFT CERTIFICATE!
THANKS, POP!
GIFT CERTIFICATE

WHAT'S THAT, VERONICA?
IT'S A SNUGGLY!
WHAT'S A SNUGGLY?!
SNUGGLY
2

THAT'S ONE OF THOSE COOL BLANKETS YOU WEAR LIKE A ROBE!
THEY'RE VERY RELAXING... MY GRANDMOTHER HAS ONE!

TRY IT ON!
MUST I?
POP'S

THIS IS ABSURD LOOKING!
HAHAHA!

YOU'RE QUITE THE FASHION PLATE!
WHO GAVE ME THIS PREPOSTEROUS GIFT?!

GUILTY!
I SHOULD'VE GUESSED!

SOON...
I'LL PICK YOU UP TONIGHT FOR THE CHRISTMAS DANCE!
I'LL BE READY!
LODGE
3

LATER...
THERE! I'M READY!
ARCHIE BETTER NOT BE LATE!

IT'S CHILLY IN HERE...
hmmm...

WELL... I COULD GIVE THIS A SHOT... AS LONG AS NOBODY IS LOOKING...
SNUGGLY

giggle
THIS IS SOOO UNFLATTERING!

BUT I HAVE TO ADMIT, IT IS COMFY!

...VERY...
...COMFY...
Z
ZZ
4

SOON...
I'M HERE TO PICK UP VERONICA, MRS. LODGE!
SHE'S IN THE LIVING ROOM, ARCHIE!

HI, RON! I'M...
Oh!
Z Z Z Z Z

SHE'S OUT COLD!
SLEEPING LIKE A BABY IN HER SNUGGLY!

I'LL WAKE HER UP!
VERONICA! ARCHIE'S HERE!
Z Z Z

JUST ONE MINUTE, MRS. LODGE!
I NEED TO GET A PICTURE OF THIS!

I HAVE TO SHOW JUGHEAD HOW MUCH VERONICA LOVES HER GIFT!
CLIK
Z
END

Jughead and his sworn nemesis Trula Twyst engage in their latest battle of wits—what kind of Christmas present to surprise each other with!

SO WHAT'S SO UNBELIEVABLE?
JUG, DID YOU GET CONKED WITH A DENSELY-PACKED SNOWBALL?
TRULA IS YOUR AVOWED ENEMY! SHE IS FLIES IN YOUR SOUP! YOU SAY SO ALL THE TIME!
BAH!
ARCH, IT'S CHRISTMAS! AT THIS TIME OF YEAR, ALL SUCH PETTINESS IS SET ASIDE!
LEAVE THE ACRIMONY TO THE OTHER ELEVEN MONTHS! CHRISTMAS IS FOR GIVING!
YOU'VE GOT SUGARPLUMS IN YOUR HEAD!
YOU'LL REMEMBER WHAT A THORN IN YOUR SIDE SHE IS, SOON ENOUGH!
GRINCH!
HMMM... AH! WHAT GIRL DOESN'T LIKE SMELLY STUFF?
Porfum
2

JUGHEAD'S SHOPPING FOR A GIFT FOR ME!
YOU'RE KIDDING! HOW DO YOU KNOW?
POP'S CHOCKLIT SHOPPE

I'VE STUDIED HIS BRAIN! I KNOW HOW HE THINKS!
WELL, YOU ARE RIVERDALE'S "POP PSYCHOLOGY" POWERHOUSE!

IT'S A CURSE SOMETIMES! I KNOW HE'LL BE BOPPING IN HERE...
PUSH

...WITH A BOTTLE OF PERFUME TO SURPRISE ME...

LOOK! JUGHEAD JUST LEFT!
NATURALLY!

HE OVERHEARD ME GUESS HIS GIFT! NOW HE'S GOING TO EXCHANGE IT!
3

SO THAT'S HOW IT IS, EH? I GOTTA BE SNEAKIER! MORE ORIGINAL!
XCHANGES
REFUNDS
OUT WITH THE PERFUME! THAT BRAINIAC WILL DIG A PSYCHOLOGY TOME!
HISTORY
THEN WHAT WILL HE DO?
HE'LL TRY TO BE UN-PREDICTABLE!
HE'LL GET ME A PSYCHOLOGY BOOK!
D'OH!
BUT HE'LL QUICKLY LEARN THAT THAT'S NO SURPRISE!
SHE READ TOO MANY BOOKS ALREADY!
SOMETHING SILLY... A GOONEY HAT!
Madam Chapeau
4

HE'LL GET WIND OF THE FACT THAT I GUESSED THE BOOK!
AND?

AND HE'LL TRY THE NOVELTY APPROACH! A SILLY HAT, I'D SAY!

AARGH! BLANKETY-BLANK BLINK BLANK!

GIMME MY MONEY BACK!

I KNOW WHEN I'M BEAT, ARCH! WHO NEEDS THIS HASSLE?

MERRY CH
5

SO WHAT'S HIS NEXT MOVE?
NONE! HE'LL GIVE UP!
GIVE UP?
YEP! HE DECIDES THE WHOLE THING IS MORE AGGRAVATING THAN IT'S WORTH! THAT'S IT!
AHEM!
MERRY CHRISTMAS, TRULA!
WHAT?
THAT'S IMPOSSIBLE! IT GOES AGAINST YOUR PSYCHOLOGICAL MAKE-UP!
Y-YOUR HEAD JUST DOESN'T WORK THAT WAY!
SINCE WHEN DOES CHRISTMAS SPIRIT COME FROM THE HEAD?
COME TO THINK OF IT... SINCE NEVER!
THE END

In this poignant Christmas tale, Riverdale's resident prankster Reggie proves he's not a Scrooge, but has a generous heart after all!

REGGIE® in Gift Horse Laugh!
WOW! THANKS FOR THE CHRISTMAS BONUS, MR. MARTIN. THIS WILL MAKE MY HOLIDAYS EXTRA MERRY!
YOU'RE WELCOME, REGGIE! EVEN THOUGH YOU CAN BE A LITTLE TOO FUNNY FOR YOUR OWN GOOD, YOU'RE STILL ONE OF MY BEST PART-TIME EMPLOYEES!
SCRIPT: MIKE PELLOWSKI
PENCILS: P. KENNEDY
INKS: KEN SELIG

HEH! HEH! DO YOU THINK WE COULD BE TWO OF THOSE SPECIAL FRIENDS HE'S TALKING ABOUT?
PERHAPS, BUT I DOUBT IT. AFTER ALL, REG ISN'T EXACTLY WELL-KNOWN FOR HIS GENEROSITY.

THAT'S TRUE, BUT IT IS THE HOLIDAY SEASON, ARCH.
I GUESS EVEN REGGIE COULD BE AFFECTED BY THE CHRISTMAS SPIRIT. WE'LL JUST HAVE TO WAIT AND SEE...

DAYS LATER, AT THE MALL...
HI, REG. ARE YOU DOING SOME LAST-MINUTE CHRISTMAS SHOPPING?
I SURE AM. I CASHED MY BONUS CHECK, AND THE LOOT IS BURNING A HOLE IN MY POCKET.
SALE

WHAT ARE YOU SHOPPING FOR?
IT'S A SECRET. I CAN ONLY SAY THIS...IT'S A GROUP OF WONDERFUL FOLKS WHO DESERVE TO BE HAPPY AT CHRISTMAS.

I HAVE TO BE GOING. 'BYE.
HMMM... I WONDER WHO HE'S TALKING ABOUT?
2

TOYS
I DON'T THINK IT'S MUCH OF A MYSTERY. REG HAS TO BE TALKING ABOUT HIS BEST FRIENDS...
...WHICH INCLUDES US.
GOSH! I DON'T KNOW ABOUT THAT, NANCY... REGGIE ISN'T THE TYPE TO SQUANDER A BONUS CHECK ON ANYONE BUT HIMSELF.

LATER...
WHEW! I GOT A LOT OF GREAT BUYS WITH MY BONUS MONEY.

HI, REG...WHAT DID YOU DO...BUY OUT THE STORES?
ALMOST, ARCH.

GOSH! YOU'RE LOADED DOWN WITH CDs, DVDs, AND...TOYS?
?
HEY, DON'T ACT SO SURPRISED. I ENJOY BUYING ALL KINDS OF GIFTS AT CHRISTMAS TIME.

AFTER ALL, I'M JUST A BIG KID AT HEART.
DO YOU MEAN TO TELL ME ALL OF THAT STUFF IS FOR YOU?
3

LET'S JUST SAY THESE GIFTS WILL MAKE MY CHRISTMAS VERY, VERY HAPPY.
REGGIE, DON'T YOU KNOW IT'S BETTER TO GIVE THAN TO RECEIVE?
YOU CELEBRATE CHRISTMAS YOUR WAY, AND I'LL CELEBRATE IT MY WAY.
HI, FELLAS. WAS THAT REGGIE MANTLE I JUST SAW, OR WAS IT SANTA CLAUS?
BELIEVE ME, IT CERTAINLY WASN'T SANTA!
MERRY CHRISTMAS TO ME. ♫ MERRY CHRISTMAS TO ME!
YOU SHOULD HAVE SEEN ALL OF THE GREAT PRESENTS REG BOUGHT...FOR HIMSELF!
HUMPH! I SHOULD HAVE KNOWN THAT REGGIE WOULD BE IMMUNE TO THE GIFT-GIVING SEASON. REGGIE WILL ALWAYS BE REGGIE.
I THINK YOU GUYS ARE BEING TOO HARSH ON REGGIE. IT IS HIS MONEY. HE CAN SPEND IT ANY WAY HE WANTS.
I GUESS YOU'RE RIGHT, ARCH. WHO ARE WE TO FAULT REG FOR HIS LACK OF CHRISTMAS SPIRIT?
4

MERRY CHRISTMAS TO ME... MERRY CHRISTMAS TO ME...
U.S. MARINES NEEDY CHILDREN CHRISTMAS DRIVE

HI, SARGE! I HAVE SOME ADDITIONAL GIFTS TO DONATE TO THE DRIVE.
HELLO, REGGIE! IT'S GOOD TO SEE YOU AGAIN. HAPPY HOLIDAYS... AND THANKS!
SERVICE

MINUTES LATER...
NOW THAT'S A WONDERFUL WAY TO PRIVATELY CELEBRATE THE HOLIDAYS. IT ALWAYS MAKES ME FEEL SPECIAL.
SNIFF!

HEY! DID YOU GUYS SEE THAT? WE SURE WERE WRONG ABOUT REGGIE. HE IS A REGULAR SANTA CLAUS AFTER ALL.
THE BEST PART IS... NO ONE KNOWS ANYTHING ABOUT THIS SECRET PART OF MY PERSONALITY!

U.S. MARINES
HO! HO! HO! HO!
AFTER ALL, REG MANTLE HAS A CERTAIN IMAGE TO MAINTAIN, EVEN AT CHRISTMAS TIME.
ARMED FORCES SERVICES
U.S. MARINES NEEDY CHILDREN CHRISTMAS DRIVE DROP-IN
PLEASE DONATE TODAY!
SNAP
CLICK!
END

Archie's FAVORITE Christmas Comics

PLAYING SANTA

Sometimes you just have to take matters into your own hands and play Santa Claus yourself! After all, Santa can't always be everywhere at once—he's got too many toys to make! Through the years, Archie, his friends, their families and the beloved Riverdale High faculty have all taken their turn playing jolly ol' Saint Nick!

WANTED: SANTA CLAUS
***Archie and Me #26*, 1969**
by Joe Edwards and Jon D'Agostino

SANTA CLAWS
***Archie Digest #248*, 2008**
by Bill Golliher, Pat Kennedy and Jim Amash

SANTA'S LITTLE HELPER
***Veronica #176*, 2007**
by Dan Parent, Jim Amash, Barry Grossman and Teresa Davidson

SANTA SHORTAGE
***Betty & Veronica #231*, 2008**
by Mike Pellowski, Jeff Shultz and Al Milgrom

It's a festive feast or famine when Archie goes from having no available volunteers to play Santa at the orphanage to way too many!

...HE SEEMS TO APPEAR TO OTHERS LIKE THIS...
ARRROAARR!
PRINCIPAL

MMMM...SO ARCHIE WANTS TO SEE ME! THAT'S A SWITCH!
MEMO

ARCHIE IS ALL I NEEDED TO TOP THINGS OFF AFTER THE WAY MY DAY STARTED!

WONDER WHAT HE WANTS ?

SNIFF! SNIFF! WHAT IS THAT FUNNY ODOR, MISS GRUNDY?
2

CAMPHOR!
CAMPHOR, MISS GRUNDY?

YES! IT'S COMING FROM THIS SANTA CLAUS COSTUME! I STORED IT IN MY CLOSET!

IT'S THE ONE YOU WORE LAST YEAR! IT'S THAT TIME OF THE YEAR, YOU KNOW!
5

AHA!
AHA, WHAT?

THAT IS WHAT ARCHIE WANTS!
WHAP!

I'LL BET HE WANTS ME TO PLAY SANTA CLAUS AGAIN?!
3

I'VE GOT A FLASH FOR ARCHIE! I'M TIRED OF BEING TAKEN FOR GRANTED!

I'M TIRED OF BEING A DOORMAT AND PEOPLE TAKING ADVANTAGE OF MY GOOD-NATURE!

I'M PUTTING MY FOOT DOWN THIS YEAR!

I'M NOT GOING TO PLAY SANTA CLAUS!!

HEY, ARCH! I'VE GOT A FLASH FOR YOU! LISTEN, ARCH...
?

GULP! HE'S RIGHT! WE HAVE IMPOSED ON HIM EVERY YEAR! HE HAS A RIGHT TO MAKE HIS OWN PLANS FOR CHRISTMAS!
4

GEE, THE KIDS AT THE ORPHANAGE WILL BE DISAPPOINTED WITH NO SANTA CLAUS!

WHY NOT GET ANOTHER SANTA CLAUS?
WHO, JUGHEAD? WHO?

MOOSE! I TELL YOU, YOU'LL BE A GOOD DEED FOR THE KIDS AT THE ORPHANAGE!

I KNOW, D-UH! BUT I HAVE A DATE WITH MIDGE AND THAT'S ONE THING I'LL NEVER BREAK!

HURUMPH, ARCHIE! I UNDERSTAND YOU WANTED TO SEE ME!
EEP!

WHAT DID YOU WANT, ARCHIE?
I-I...(ER)... JUST W-WANTED TO...
5

...TO WISH YOU A MERRY CHRISTMAS!

?
MERRY CHRISTMAS??
?

...ER... THAT'S ALL, ARCHIE? JUST MERRY CHRISTMAS?!?

Y-YES SIR! THAT'S ALL!
? ?

T-H-A-T'S A-L-L??
GULP!

HE DIDN'T ASK ME TO PLAY SANTA CLAUS...
6

GULP! WHAT'S THE MATTER WITH ME? I'M KIND... LOVABLE... JOLLY... A PERFECT ROLY-POLY FIGURE FOR SANTA!

I'VE GOT A KIND, WARM SANTA CLAUS LAUGH...

HO HO HO
HO HO HO

GULP! WHO AM I KIDDING? LATELY, I HAVEN'T REALLY BEEN SO JOLLY!!

I'VE BEEN CROSS AND GRUMPY! MAYBE ARCHIE IS RIGHT IN NOT ASKING ME TO PLAY SANTA!

WELL, I'LL SHOW HIM... NO!! I'LL PROVE TO HIM I'M A PERFECT SANTA!
7

ER... HURUMPH!
HO HO HO...
?

HO HO HO!!

SMILE, ARCHIE! CHEER UP! LIFE IS GREAT! HO HO HO!!

HUMMPH! HE SAYS SMILE! HA!

HE'S BUGGING ME ABOUT SMILING WHILE I'M GOING NUTS TRYING TO FIND A SANTA CLAUS!

BUT WHO? WHO, JUGHEAD?
DON'T LOOK AT ME LIKE THAT, ARCHIE!
8

HOLD STILL, JUG! THE PILLOW KEEPS FALLING OUT!
I DON'T THINK A SKINNY SANTA IS IN KEEPING WITH THE CHARACTER!
PLOP!

HOW DO I LOOK??

YECH!

I GUESS THERE'S ONLY ONE THING LEFT TO DO...

WHAT'S THAT, ARCH?

I'LL PLAY THE PART OF SANTA CLAUS!
9

THAT NIGHT AT THE ORPHANAGE...
ALL RIGHT, CHILDREN! GUESS WHO IS HERE TONIGHT TO PAY YOU A VISIT ?

SANTA CLAUS!
YOU'RE RIGHT, BOYS AND GIRLS! HERE HE COMES!

WHAT TH...?? THERE ARE THREE OF THEM!!

MOOSE ?
MR. WEATHERBEE ?
ARCHIE ?

D-UH, MIDGE SAID SHE'D NEVER FORGIVE ME IF I DIDN'T PLAY SANTA!
AHEM! AND I WOULDN'T FORGIVE MYSELF IF I DIDN'T EITHER!

GULP! HOW ARE YOU GOING TO EXPLAIN THIS TO THE KIDS ?
I'VE GOT IT!

3 SANTAS NO WAITING

PSSST... ARCHIE, WE FORGOT SOMEONE VERY IMPORTANT!
WHO ?

Merry Christmas
DEAR READER
12
END

'Twas the week before Christmas and all through the mall, not a creature was stirring—except for all the pets who came to the department store to get their photos taken with Santa Archie!

WOW! ARCHIE... ER... SANTA, THIS SHOULD BE ONE HOLIDAY JOB THAT'S FUN!
SURE, BETTY... IT'S GOING TO BE A PIECE OF CAKE!

SOON...
FIRST CUSTOMER, PLEASE!
OH, GOODY! THAT'S US!

WHERE'S YOUR PET?
IN THIS BASKET! HE'S A LITTLE NERVOUS WITH THE OTHER ANIMALS AROUND...

...EXCEPT FOR THE SMALL ONES! HE'D LIKE TO EAT THEM!
HSSSS
A SNAKE!!

MAYBE HE CAN TELL ME WHAT HE'D LIKE FROM THERE!
HSSSS
NO, SILLY! WE GET A PHOTO OF 'SNUGGLES' WITH SANTA EVERY YEAR!
2

UH, SNUGGLES IS WRAPPING AROUND ME!
OF COURSE, SANTA! MY PYTHON LOVES TO GIVES PEOPLE 'HUGS'!

ARCHIE, SMILE SO I CAN TAKE THE PICTURE!
GRUNT THAT'S NOT EASY WHEN YOU'RE GETTING SQUEEZED!

GOT IT!
SNUGGLES, YOU MUST REALLY LIKE THIS SANTA! YOU'RE HOLDING ON TIGHT!
URF!

NEXT, WE HAVE A DOG FOR YOU, SANTA!
THANK GOODNESS, SOMETHING ORDINARY! HERE BOY!

EEP!
WOOF!

ARE YOU OKAY?
!
I THINK SO, BUT I COULD DROWN IF THIS KEEPS UP!
3

CUT IT OUT, MAJOR! SANTA KNOWS YOU'VE BEEN A GOOD BOY!
THANKS!
SLURP

OKAY, HOLD THAT POSE!
URF! EASIER SAID THAN DONE!

SAY HELLO TO SANTA, MR. PICKLES!
WHAT A CUTE NAME YOU HAVE, KITTY!

ROWRR
CALM DOWN, BOY! WE'RE GETTING OUR PICTURE TAKEN!

OW! HE'S DIGGING HIS CLAWS INTO 'CLAUS'!!
HSS!
THAT JUST MEANS HE'S COMFORTABLE!
SMILE!

COULD YOU FIND ME SOMETHING SMALL AND PLEASANT FOR A CHANGE?!
4

YOU'RE IN LUCK! THE NEXT YOUNG MAN HAS TWO HAMSTERS!
THEY DON'T GET MUCH SMALLER THAN THAT!

OKAY... LOOK AT THE CAMERA!
OUCH!
ONE JUST BIT ME!!

HEY! THEY JUST DUCKED INTO MY COSTUME!
OH, DEAR!

HOW CAN I GET A PHOTO WITH THEM INSIDE YOUR CLOTHES?
BELIEVE ME, KID-- NOT MY IDEA!!

WAHHH!
SANTA WON'T GIVE MY PETS BACK!!
I'LL USE SOME OF THESE HAMSTER SNACKS TO LURE THEM OUT!
shake
shake

IT WORKED!
UH-OH! BUT HERE COMES SOMEONE ELSE!!
5

EEP!!
MEOWRR!
NO, MR. PICKLES! NO!
MAJOR! COME BACK!!

MEOWR
ARFF
SQUEAL SQUEAL
GROWLL
HO HOHO

SOON...
THANK GOODNESS OUR PETS ARE OKAY!
YES, THAT WAS QUITE A BIT OF EXCITEMENT! BUT THOSE THINGS HAPPEN, RIGHT, ARCHIE!?

ARCHIE? WHERE DID YOU GO? WE'RE NOT IN THE DOG HOUSE OVER THAT!

I AM!
AND I REFUSE TO COME OUT UNTIL AFTER CHRIST-MAS!!
DOG HOUSE SALE
FIDO
END

Veronica secretly takes a "Santa's helper" position to be closer to department store Santa Archie... who unbeknownst to Veronica has left early for the day!

Veronica SANTA'S Little Helper

ARCHIE, WE BARELY SPENT ANY TIME TOGETHER THIS CHRISTMAS SEASON.

SORRY, RON. BUT I'VE HAD TO WORK! I NEED MONEY FOR CHRISTMAS GIFTS.

ARE YOU STILL PLAYING SANTA IN THE MALL?
YES! TODAY AT 2:00.

BUT GET THERE EARLY SO YOU DON'T HAVE TO STAND IN LINE!
AND BRING YOUR CHRISTMAS LIST!

LATER...
YOU LOOK GREAT, ARCHIE!
THANKS! I THINK I NEED ANOTHER PILLOW!

I HAVE TO GO OUT THERE.
GOOD LUCK!

HEY, HONEY! WHAT ARE YOU DOING LATER?
NOT GOING OUT WITH YOU, DWEEB!

GO HELP SANTA LIKE YOU'RE SUPPOSED TO!
LATER, CUTIE!
2

SO...
ARCHIE'S SO BUSY, I'LL NEVER SEE HIM TODAY!

HEY, WHAT'S THIS?
"HIRING SANTA ASSISTANTS"?
NOW WE'RE TALKING!
HIRING SANTA ASSISTANTS
INQUIRE WITHIN

YOU'RE HIRED, VERONICA!
KEEP IN MIND, YOU'LL HAVE TO STAND BY SANTA ALL DAY.
DRESSI ROOM

I THINK I CAN HANDLE THAT.
HERE. PUT YOUR OUTFIT ON AND BEGIN WORK.
RESSING ROOM

SANTA, YOU HAVE A PHONE CALL.
HELLO?
ARCHIE, I HATE TO BOTHER YOU AT WORK, BUT WE NEED YOU AT HOME!
A WATER PIPE BURST AND DAD NEEDS YOU!
3

ARCHIE, IF THERE'S A PROBLEM, PHIL CAN COVER FOR YOU!
THANKS, BOSS!
DRESSING ROOM

HERE, PHIL! PUT ARCHIE'S SANTA OUTFIT ON!
I HAVE A NEW ASSISTANT ON HER WAY OUT!
DRESSING ROOM

SOON...
HI, SANTA! IT'S ME, YOUR FAVORITE HELPER!
SHE THINKS I'M ARCHIE!

YOU'VE BEEN WORKING HARD!
LET ME GIVE YOU A HUG, SANTA!

HAS MY POOPSY WOOPSY BEEN WORKING HARD?
UH-HUH!
GAG!

SOON...
IT'S FINALLY SLOWED DOWN!
NOW IT'S MY TURN!
4

HO! HO! HO! AND WHAT WOULD YOU LIKE FOR CHRISTMAS?
YOU CAN KNOCK OFF THE SANTA VOICE. NOBODY'S AROUND, ARCHIE.
NOW LET ME PULL DOWN THAT BEARD AND GIVE YOU A KISS...
Uh-oh!

GAK!! YOU'RE NOT ARCHIE! YOU'RE THAT TROLL, PHIL!
ARCHIE HAD TO LEAVE!

YUCK! TO THINK I COZIED UP TO YOU!
COME BACK! I DIDN'T GET MY KISS YET!

STAY AWAY, YOU CREEP!
JUST ONE LITTLE KISS!
MY, THESE HOLIDAY DISPLAYS HAVE CHANGED SINCE I WAS A KID!
END

Throwing a Christmas party for needy kids without a Santa Claus? Better find a replacement... or two... or three... quick!

Betty and Veronica in Santa SHORTAGE

THIS WILL BE THE BEST CHRISTMAS PARTY FOR NEEDY CHILDREN WE'VE EVER HAD. THANKS FOR COORDINATING THE EVENT, GIRLS!

IT WAS OUR PLEASURE, MRS. MARTIN. EXCUSE ME, MY CELL PHONE IS RINGING!

BR'I'ING

RIVERDALE LADIES CLUB CHRISTMAS CELEBRATION

SCRIPT: MIKE PELLOWSKI
PENCILS: JEFF SHULTZ
INKS: AL MILGROM

RELAX! I'LL JUST FIND SOMEBODY ELSE!
FINDING A SUBSTITUTE SANTA ON SHORT NOTICE WON'T BE EASY! JOLLY GUYS IN RED SUITS ARE IN BIG DEMAND THIS TIME OF YEAR!

AFTER MANY CALLS...
GOSH! YOU WERE RIGHT, BETTY! I COULDN'T FIND ANYONE SUITABLE AT ANY PRICE. WE COULD SETTLE FOR A SECOND RATE SANTA, BUT WE MIGHT GET A GRINCH!

WE CAN'T CHANCE THAT, RON! A BAD SANTA COULD RUIN CHRISTMAS FOR THE KIDS!
THEN WHAT ARE WE GOING TO DO?!

WE CAN TRY ASKING OUR FRIENDS. HEY! ARCHIE WOULD MAKE A GREAT SANTA! HE'S FRIENDLY AND JOLLY!
I'LL CALL HIM THIS INSTANT!

HO! HO! HO! HELLO! OH, HI RON! WHAT'S UP? ME PLAY SANTA FOR SOME NEEDY KIDS? SURE! WHEN?
2

Uh-OH! THERE'S A SNAG! THE BASKETBALL TEAM IS PLAYING IN A HOLIDAY TOURNAMENT IN SOUTH SIDE THAT NIGHT. I WON'T BE ABLE TO MAKE IT!
NEEDY KIDS?

Sigh! THANKS ANYWAY, ARCHIE!

ARCHIE CAN'T DO IT... NOW WHAT?
I'D ASK MY DAD, BUT HE'S ON A BUSINESS TRIP! HOW ABOUT YOUR FATHER?

HE'S AWAY UNTIL CHRISTMAS EVE. HEY, HOW ABOUT BIG MOOSE? HE'S NOT ON THE BASKETBALL SQUAD THIS YEAR!
I'LL GIVE HIM A RING!

BETTY PHONES MOOSE AND EXPLAINS...
I'D LOVE TO PLAY SANTA CLAUS FOR NEEDY KIDS, BUT I CAN'T. I DIDN'T GO OUT FOR BASKETBALL SO I COULD WRESTLE THIS YEAR!
NEEDY KIDS?
15
POP'S

I HAVE A BIG WRESTLING MATCH ON THAT DAY.
SORRY, BETTY!
3

HEY, DILLY! HOW ABOUT PLAYING SANTA FOR SOME NEEDY KIDS!?

THAT SOUNDS LIKE FUN. WHEN WOULD YOU NEED ME?

RON EXPLAINS AND TELLS DILTON THE DATE OF THE PARTY...

GOLLY! WE HAVE A DEBATE THAT NIGHT! I'M CAPTAIN OF THE TEAM ... I *HAVE* TO BE THERE!

WE UNDERSTAND, DILLY... IT *IS* SHORT NOTICE!

THE NIGHT OF THE PARTY...

LOOK! THERE'S A SECOND SANTA!
AND A THIRD! AND A FOURTH!

I RECOGNIZE THEM NOW! THAT'S MR. ANDREWS, THAT'S POP TATE, AND THAT'S MR. WEATHER-BEE!
YOU'RE RIGHT! BUT WHO'S THAT SANTA?

WOW! LOOK AT ALL THE SANTAS! THIS IS THE BEST CHRISTMAS EVER!!
HO! HO! HO!

AFTER THE PARTY ENDS...
THANKS FOR HELPING, EVERYONE. THE KIDS HAD A GREAT TIME! SAY, DOES ANYONE KNOW WHERE THAT OTHER SANTA WENT?
HE WAS A MYSTERY MAN! HE JUST HANDED OUT HIS GIFTS AND VANISHED, LIKE MAGIC!

RON, YOU DON'T SUPPOSE HE WAS...
WHO KNOWS, BETTY... ALL I KNOW IS, THE MORE SANTAS WE HAVE, THE MERRIER THE WORLD WILL BE!
END

Veronica's Christmas Card

Archie's FAVORITE Christmas Comics

SANTA AND HIS ELVES

Riverdale has welcomed a lot of special visitors over the past seven decades, including the jolly ol' man in red himself... Santa Claus! The magic and whimsy of Ol' St. Nick and his elves are alive in Riverdale every Christmas season, much to the delight of Archie and his pals! But it's not just a one way street—Archie and the gang have also taken quite a few trips to visit their friend at the North Pole, too!

PLAYING SANTA
***Jughead & Friends Digest #35*, 2010**
by Mike Pellowski, Fernando Ruiz,
Al Milgrom, Jon D'Agostino
and Barry Grossman

SURPRISE PRESENTS
***Archie Digest #248,* 2008**
by George Gladir, Jeff Shultz,
Rich Koslowski, Jack Morelli
and Barry Grossman

PIZZA AND GOOD CHEER
***Jughead's Double Digest #145,* 2009**
by Mike Pellowski, Fernando Ruiz,
Al Nickerson, Jack Morelli
and Barry Grossman

When ailing Ol' Kris Kringle needs extra help delivering presents, Jughead trades in his trademark crown cap for a genuine Santa hat! But can even Jughead find his baby sister the elusive "Laugh-a-Lot Elroy" doll that's been sold out for months?

Jughead® in "PLAYING SANTA"

⁝SNIFF! SNIFF!⁝

GOSH, MOM AND DAD, YOU TWO SOUND TERRIBLE!

AH-CHOO!

Script: MIKE PELLOWSKI Pencils: FERNANDO RUIZ Inks: AL MILGROM Letters: JON D'AGOSTINO Colors: BARRY GROSSMAN

OH WELL, WE CAN'T LET HOW WE FEEL RUIN JELLYBEAN'S HOLIDAY!
I KNOW! JELLYBEAN WILL BE DISAPPOINTED ENOUGH WHEN SHE OPENS HER PRESENTS TOMORROW!

HUH? WHAT DO YOU MEAN?
WE COULDN'T GET WHAT SHE WANTED THE MOST! ALL THE STORES ARE SOLD OUT OF LAUGH-A-LOT ELROY DOLLS!

WE EVEN SEARCHED THE NET WITH NO LUCK! I DON'T THINK THERE'S A SINGLE LAUGH-A-LOT ELROY DOLL ON SALE ANYWHERE!
JELLYBEAN WILL BE UPSET, LAUGH-A-LOT ELROY IS THE STAR OF HER FAVORITE EDUCATIONAL TV SHOW!

SHE LOVES THAT CUTE LITTLE GUY!
TEE-HEE-HEE! I'M ELROY!
ELROY-O's

I SURE HOPE THIS DOESN'T AFFECT HOW JELLYBEAN FEELS ABOUT SANTA CLAUS!
AH-AHH... CHOOO!
2

YOU BOTH LOOK LIKE YOU CAN USE THE REST!

THANKS, SON! WE'LL TAKE YOU UP ON THAT OFFER!

DON'T FORGET TO SAMPLE THE MILK AND COOKIES JELLYBEAN LEFT OUT FOR SANTA!

A SHORT TIME LATER...

YAWN! I HOPE JELLYBEAN ISN'T TOO DISAPPOINTED WHEN SHE FINDS OUT SANTA DIDN'T BRING HER LAUGH-A-LOT ELROY! YAWN!

3

ARE YOU SURE **HE'S** THE ONE SANTA PICKED?

YES! JUGHEAD JONES ALWAYS BELIEVED IN SANTA WHEN HE WAS YOUNG...HE STILL KEEPS THE SPIRIT OF SANTA CLAUS ALIVE EVEN TODAY!
OKAY... LET'S POP INSIDE AND GET BUSY!
POOF!

HEY, JUGHEAD! WAKE UP! YOU'VE GOT WORK TO DO! SANTA NEEDS YOUR HELP!
HUH? WHO? WHAT?

SANTA NEEDS *MY* HELP?
THAT'S RIGHT! HE'S TOO ILL TO FINISH HIS ROUNDS! HE NEEDS YOU TO DELIVER PRESENTS TO RIVERDALE!
4

LOOK AT ME! HOW CAN I PINCH HIT FOR SANTA?
DON'T WORRY! WE'LL FIX THAT WITH A LITTLE ELF MAGIC!
SNAP!
POOF!
HE LOOKS BETTER, BUT HE'S STILL TOO SKINNY! PLUMP HIM UP A BIT!
RIGHT!
SNAP!
HOLY SMOKE! THEY ALWAYS SAID MY EATING HABITS WOULD CATCH UP WITH ME SOME DAY!
POOF!
BOING!
RELAX, JUG, YOU'LL SLIM DOWN WHEN WE'RE DONE!
WOW!
CLIMB ABOARD, JUG... I MEAN, SANTA JUGHEAD!
5

ON DONNER! ON BLINTZES!
THAT'S BLITZEN! PLEASE KEEP YOUR MIND ON THE JOB AND OFF OF FOOD!
YEOW!

HO! HO! HO! HERE WE GO!
SLOW DOWN, SANTA JUG! OUR FIRST STOP IS JUST AHEAD!

HEY, THIS IS ARCHIE'S HOUSE!
THAT'S RIGHT! ARCHIE ANDREWS HAS BEEN EXTRA GOOD THIS YEAR!

GULP! HEY GUYS, CAN'T I JUST USE THE FRONT DOOR?
SORRY, SANTA ALWAYS SLIDES DOWN THE CHIMNEY! NOW GET GOING!
6

OUCH! I NEED TO WORK ON MY LANDINGS!
WHUMP!
YIKES! I'D BETTER BE QUIET, ARCH IS SNOOZING ON THE COUCH!

AFTER JUG PUTS PRESENTS UNDER THE TREE...
NOW IT'S BACK UP THE CHIMNEY!
WHOOSH!
HURRY UP, SANTA JUG...WE HAVE OTHER STOPS TO MAKE!
GIVE ME A BREAK, MR. ELF! I'M NOT USED TO POPPING UP AND DOWN LIKE THIS! I FEEL LIKE A PIECE OF TOAST!

ONE BY ONE SANTA JUG POPS IN HOUSES IN RIVERDALE INCLUDING THE HOMES OF HIS OTHER FRIENDS...
JINGLE BELLS, REGGIE SMELLS, SANTA'S ON HIS WAY!

AT THE DOILEYS' HOUSE, DILTON GETS A NEW LAP TOP...
HO! HO! HO! IN THIS CASE THE CREATURE THAT'S STIRRING IS A COMPUTER MOUSE!
MOOSE MASON GETS EXERCISE EQUIPMENT...
NOW MOOSE CAN BUILD HIMSELF UP FROM HIS MUSCLE HEAD TO HIS MUSCLE TOES!

AT BETTY'S HOUSE, SANTA JUGHEAD GETS TO ENJOY A BONUS...
YUM! BETTY BAKES THE WORLD'S BEST CHRISTMAS COOKIES!
HA, WE WONDERED WHAT WAS TAKING YOU SO LONG!

JUG LEAVES GIFTS FOR EVERYONE IN RIVERDALE...
CHUCK WILL LOVE THE WATER-COLOR SET I LEFT FOR HIM!
HEY, YOU'RE GETTING REALLY GOOD AT POPPING OUT OF CHIMNEYS, SANTA JUG!
WHEN SANTA'S ROUNDS ARE FINALLY COMPLETE, JUG HEADS HOME...
MERRY CHRISTMAS TO ALL, AND TO ALL A GOOD NIGHT!
8

BACK AT JUGHEAD'S HOUSE...
YOU DID A WONDERFUL JOB, JUG! SANTA WILL BE PROUD OF YOU!
THANKS, TELL SANTA I HOPE HE FEELS BETTER! NOW I HAVE TO SIT DOWN... POPPING IN AND OUT OF CHIMNEYS IS EXHAUSTING!
:YAWN!: I'M EVEN TOO TIRED TO FINISH THOSE COOKIES AND MILK!
GOSH! HE MUST REALLY BE BEAT!
OKAY! LET'S TURN HIM BACK TO NORMAL AND GET THE PACKAGE FOR YOU-KNOW-WHO!
OKAY!
THE NEXT MORNING...
MERRY CHRISTMAS!
YIPPIE!
:SNORT!: W-WHAT?
9

JUGHEAD? ARE YOU STILL DOWN HERE?
GOSH! I GUESS I NODDED OFF...SLEPT HERE ALL NIGHT! BOY! DID I EVER HAVE A WACKY DREAM!
SANTA! SANTA!
YOU BOTH LOOK MUCH BETTER TODAY!
THANKS! THAT EXTRA SLEEP DID US A WORLD OF GOOD!
JELLYBEAN WANTS TO OPEN A GIFT! WHO'S THAT FROM?
GEE, I DON'T KNOW! THE BOX DOESN'T LOOK FAMILIAR!
THE LABEL SAYS IT'S TO JELLYBEAN...FROM SANTA CLAUS!
SANTA!
TEE-HEE-HEE! HI, I'M LAUGH-A-LOT ELROY!
10

LAUGH-A-LOT ELROY? B-BUT WHO? HOW?

HUMM... I THINK I KNOW THE ANSWER!

YOU PLAYED SANTA CLAUS AFTER WE WENT TO BED LAST NIGHT, DIDN'T YOU, JUGHEAD?

WHO ME?

:GASP!: I-I'M NOT SURE! I THOUGHT IT WAS ALL A DREAM! IT REALLY DIDN'T HAPPEN...OR DID IT?

Progress comes to the North Pole: Santa has his first-ever female elf, Lisa—and she invents Santa's first-ever website! All is not merry, however, when Lisa decides the boys need a more romantic present than video games!

Archie & FRIENDS in The SURPRISE PRESENTS

LISA IS MY VERY FIRST FEMALE ELF! AND SHE'S COME UP WITH AN EXCELLENT IDEA!

SANTA'S OWN WEB PAGE... WHERE BOYS AND GIRLS CAN ORDER THEIR OWN CHRISTMAS GIFTS ONLINE!

Santa's GIFTS GALORE

Script: GEORGE GLADIR Pencils: JEFF SHULTZ Inks: RICH KOSLOWSKI Letters: JACK MORELLI Colors: BARRY GROSSMAN

Hmm... THIS IS A VERY RADICAL DEPARTURE FROM WHAT WE USUALLY DO...
LET'S GIVE IT A VERY LIMITED TRIAL RUN TO SEE IF IT WORKS!

WE'LL CONFINE THE OFFER TO A VERY SMALL TOWN...
...LET'S SEE HOW IT PANS OUT IN RIVERDALE, USA!

JUG, YOU'RE NOT GOING TO BELIEVE WHAT JUST POPPED UP ON MY SCREEN!
RIVERDALE

SANTA NOW HAS HIS VERY OWN WEB PAGE!
SOMEONE'S PUTTING YOU ON!
RIVERDALE

EVERY GUY AND GAL WILL NOW BE ABLE TO TELL SANTA DIRECTLY WHAT THEY WANT FOR CHRIST-MAS -- AND THEY'LL GET IT!
MYSELF, I THINK IT'S SOME HACKER'S IDEA OF A BIG BODACIOUS SCAM!
2

JUG, WHAT HAVE WE GOT TO LOSE?
IT SAYS NO MONEY OR CONFIDENTIAL INFO IS REQUIRED!
IT DOES?

WOW! I CAN THINK OF OVER A HUNDRED VIDEO GAMES I'D LIKE AS A PRESENT!
Hmm... ME TOO! WITH SOME SNACKIES THROWN IN FOR GOOD MEASURE!

WELL, LISA, THE BIG COUNTDOWN IS ON... JUST ONE MORE DAY UNTIL CHRISTMAS!
DECEMBER

SO, GIRL, HOW ARE THE ORDERS COMING IN?
Oh, THIS IS SO UNEXPECTED, HERMAN!

THE BOYS IN RIVERDALE ARE ASKING FOR VIDEO GAMES, VIDEO GAMES, AND MORE VIDEO GAMES!

AND WHAT'S WRONG WITH THAT?
I'LL TELL YOU WHAT'S WRONG WITH THAT! ALL THOSE GAMES WILL MAKE THOSE BOYS NEGLECT THEIR GIRLFRIENDS!
3

BUT THOSE VIDEO GAMES ARE WHAT THE BOYS WANT!
IT'S WHAT THE BOYS THINK THEY WANT!

I'M GOING TO CHANGE THE GIFT LIST FOR ALL THOSE BOYS!
BUT LISA, YOU NEED SANTA'S PERMISSION TO DO THAT!

IT'S TOO LATE TO CONTACT HIM... SANTA'S ALREADY ON HIS RUN! ...AND HE TURNS OFF HIS CELL ON CHRISTMAS EVE!

I'LL HAVE A DOZEN ELVES DELIVER A SPECIAL GAME TO THE BOYS IN RIVERDALE! ... ONE THAT SHOULD SATISFY BOTH BOYS AND GIRLS!

BUT, LISA! YOU CAN'T DO THAT!!
SORRY, OL' SPORTS! IT'S ALREADY A DONE DEAL!
BOOP
4

CHRISTMAS MORNING!
AT LONG LAST! TODAY IS THE LONG AWAITED DAY!!

ALL THOSE VIDEO GAMES AND SNACKYPOOS ARE JUST WAITING FOR YOU, JUGGIE-BOY!!

?! ALL I GOT WAS THIS ONE BOX?! I WONDER WHAT'S INSIDE...

? IT'S JUST AN EMPTY BOTTLE... AND A SET OF INSTRUCTIONS...

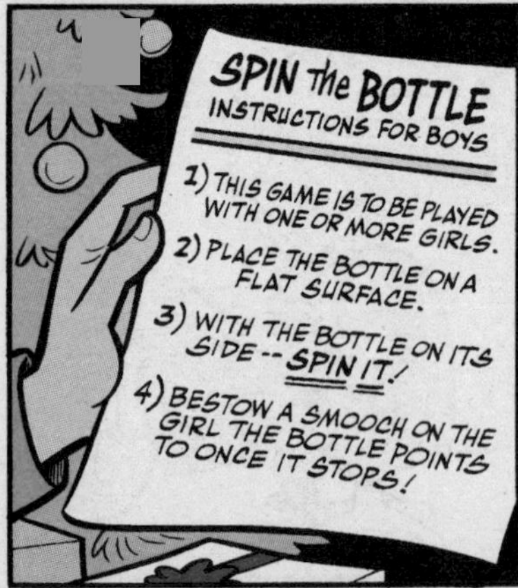
SPIN the BOTTLE
INSTRUCTIONS FOR BOYS
1) THIS GAME IS TO BE PLAYED WITH ONE OR MORE GIRLS.
2) PLACE THE BOTTLE ON A FLAT SURFACE.
3) WITH THE BOTTLE ON ITS SIDE -- SPIN IT!
4) BESTOW A SMOOCH ON THE GIRL THE BOTTLE POINTS TO ONCE IT STOPS!

MAN! WHAT A HUMONGOUS RIP-OFF!!
I WONDER IF ARCHIE GOT SWINDLED, TOO!!
5

YOU'LL FIND ARCHIE IN THE LIVING ROOM WITH SOME FRIENDS!

ARCHIE! DID YOU SEE WHAT SANTA DARED GIVE US INSTEAD OF VIDEO GAMES?!
YEAH... AND WHO IS COMPLAINING?

WELL, SANTA! OUR DAY IS FINALLY OVER!
NOT QUITE! WE'LL FLY OVER RIVERDALE AND CHECK OUT HOW THINGS ARE GOING!

HERE COME A COUPLE OF RIVERDALE KIDS NOW...
WE'LL SOON SEE HOW THEY LIKED THEIR WEB PAGE PRESENTS!

HELP! SANTA IS ONE BIG, BIG FRAUD!!
JUGGIE... THE GAME! WE HAVE TO PLAY THE GAME!!

SO, BOSS, WHAT DO YOU THINK?
DOESN'T LOOK LIKE I'LL BE SPENDING NEXT CHRISTMAS VACATIONING IN HAWAII-!
END

Take Jughead, some pizzas, and a giving heart. Now mix it all up with good cheer and what have you got? A yuletide tale that will warm your heart... and your belly!

YUM! AN OCCASIONAL SLICE OF PIZZA WOULD BE A WELCOME CHANGE!
WHY DON'T YOU PUT IT ON YOUR WISH LIST FOR SANTA? COME ON, LET'S EAT!

GOSH! DID YOU HEAR THAT, NANCY?
YES, JUG. WHY?

IT MAKES ME FEEL GUILTY... I WAS PLANNING ON STOPPING FOR PIZZA ON MY WAY HOME!
DON'T FEEL THAT WAY, JUG! YOU DONATE YOUR TIME AND WHAT MONEY YOU CAN TO HELP THE HOME-LESS!

YOU'RE NOT SANTA CLAUS, YOU KNOW. GO ENJOY YOUR PIZZA!
WELL, OKAY... I'LL TRY TO...

OOPS! EXCUSE ME, SIR!
BUMP
OOF! IT WAS ENTIRELY MY FAULT, YOUNG MAN...!

IF YOU COULD USE A GOOD MEAL, THERE'S PLENTY OF FOOD INSIDE! WE'LL BE SERVING FREE TURKEY DINNERS OVER THE HOLIDAYS!
ACTUALLY, I WAS THINK-ING OF GOING HOME FOR THE HOLIDAYS!

2

THE PROBLEM IS, I DON'T HAVE ENOUGH MONEY TO MAKE THE TRIP!
HUH? JUST A MINUTE!
IS THIS ENOUGH TO GET YOU HOME?
MORE THAN ENOUGH! THIS'LL COVER ALL OF MY TRAVEL EXPENSES! THANK YOU!
YOU'RE VERY WELCOME! GEE, I DID A GOOD DEED AND STILL HAVE ENOUGH LEFT OVER FOR ONE SLICE OF PIZZA!
MAYBE I CAN RETURN YOUR KIND-NESS! IF YOU WANT GOOD PIZZA, TRY NOEL'S JUST AROUND THE CORNER!
I SEND EVERYONE WHO PASSES MY GENEROSITY TEST THERE! I KNOW YOU'LL LIKE IT!
GOODBYE! AND THANKS FOR THE TIP ABOUT NOEL'S! I'VE NEVER EATEN THERE!
WOW! THIS PLACE MUST BE GOOD! LOOK AT ALL THE PEOPLE GOING IN!
NOEL'S P
CELEBRATING OUR 25
NOEL'S PIZZA
3

GOSH! I'M SORRY, SIR! I'M BUMPING INTO EVERYONE TONIGHT!
WATCH YOUR STEP, BUB! WHERE DO YOU THINK YOU'RE GOING ?!
BUMP
I'M HEADED INTO THE PIZZA PARLOR!
OH, NO! YOU CAN'T GO IN THERE JUST YET!

WHY NOT ?! OTHER PEOPLE ARE GOING IN THERE!
ORDERS! HMM... OKAY, YOU CAN GO IN NOW!

BY THE WAY, MERRY CHRISTMAS, BUB!
AH, THANKS! SAME TO YOU!
WHAT AN ODD LITTLE FELLOW!

YAHOO!!
CONGRATULATIONS! YOU'RE CUSTOMER NUMBER ONE MILLION!!
ARE YOU EVER LUCKY YOU CAME IN WHEN YOU DID!
I AM?!!
TOOT
SNAP
PIZZA
4

YOU WIN THREE FREE PIZZAS PER WEEK FOR SIX MONTHS! WHAT'S YOUR NAME AND ADDRESS!
I DO?! WHAT A GREAT HOLIDAY GIFT! MY NAME IS JUGHEAD JONES AND I LIVE AT--

Hmmm... CAN I DO ANYTHING I WANT WITH THOSE PIZZAS?
OF COURSE! JUST NAME IT!

I'D LIKE TO HAVE THEM DELIVERED TO THE GOOD NEIGHBOR KITCHEN EVERY FRIDAY NIGHT FOR SIX MONTHS!
IT WILL BE OUR PLEASURE TO DO THAT! IS THERE ANYTHING ELSE?

YES! I'D LIKE ONE SLICE OF PIZZA, WHICH I WILL PAY FOR!
COMING RIGHT UP, MR. JONES!

NOEL'S PIZZA
BOY, DO I FEEL GOOD! IT'S STRANGE THE WAY THINGS HAPPEN DURING THE HOLIDAYS!
5

THE FOLLOWING EVENING AT THE JONES' HOME...
Ding Dong
I'LL GET THE DOOR WHILE YOU FIX ME A SNACK, MOM! I'M STARVING!
OKAY, SON!

SPECIAL PIZZA DELIVERY, BUB!
HUH? WOW! LOOK AT THE SIZE OF THAT PIE! UN-FORTUNATELY, NO ONE HERE ORDERED IT!
ONES

JUST TAKE IT, BUB! IT'S ALL PAID FOR, AND I CAN'T STAND HERE CHATTING! I HAVE OTHER PLACES TO GO!
GOSH! THE DELIVERY SLIP DOES SAY J. JONES! BUT WHERE DID IT COME FROM?

NORTH POLE PIZZA?! OH, NO! IT COULDN'T BE FROM YOU-KNOW-WHO... COULD IT?!
NORTH POLE PIZZA
HO! HO! HO! MERRY CHRISTMAS TO ALL!
JINGLE JINGLE
THE END

Archie's
Christmas Card
JUST THOUGHT I'D DROP IN TO WISH YOU A VERY MERRY CHRISTMAS and a HAPPY NEW YEAR!
Archie

Archie's FAVORITE Christmas Comics

SANTA'S SPRITES

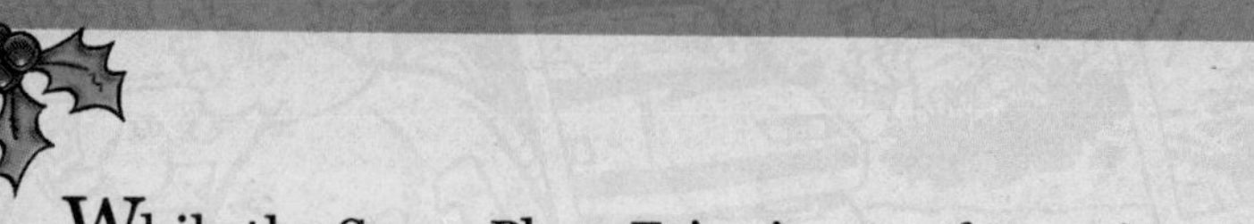

While the Sugar Plum Fairy is one of Santa's most magical sprites, Jingles the Elf is both magical and mischievous! He's accident-prone and easily agitated... but in true Christmas spirit, never for long! No matter how big the mess, and whether or not Archie and his friends created the chaos or Jingles' himself stirred the pot, he always manages to set things straight with a little humor, a little whimsy and a whole lot of magic!

A JOB FOR JINGLES
Archie Giant Series #10, 1961
by Frank Doyle, Dan DeCarlo, Rudy Lapick
and Vincent DeCarlo

RETURN OF JINGLES
Archie Giant Series #20, 1963
by Frank Doyle, Dan DeCarlo, Rudy Lapick
and Vincent DeCarlo

SEASON OF MAGIC
Archie Giant Series #158, 1969
by Frank Doyle, Bob White and Bill Yoshida

TREED
Archie Giant Series #150, 1968
by Frank Doyle, Al Hartley and Bill Yoshida

JINGLES ROCKS
Archie & Friends #21, 2012
by Bill Golliher, Rudy Lapick, Barry Grossman
and Bill Yoshida

It's a momentous occasion: the first time Archie and his friends ever met Jingles the Elf! Of course, since only the kids can see him, all the adults think the teens have eaten too many candy canes! Of course, that won't stop Jingles from working a little holiday magic!

Archie in "A Job for Jingles"

W-WHO ARE YOU?

I'M JINGLES!

(YAWN) - WHAT YOU ARE, BUDDY, IS A FIGMENT OF MY IMAGINATION!
TSK, TSK!

TALK LIKE THAT LEADS TO A STOCKING FULL OF COAL, PAL!

MAYBE SOME FOOD WILL CLEAR MY HEAD!

GREAT! I'M STARVED!
LONG WALK FROM THE NORTH POLE, EH?

PANCAKES, ARCHIE?
FINE, MOM!

SEE? I KNEW YOU WEREN'T REALLY THERE!
MOM DIDN'T EVEN NOTICE YOU!

BOY! ARE YOU DUMB! BROWNIES CAN'T BE SEEN BY ADULTS!
PARDON MY IGNORANCE! AND PASS THE SYRUP!
SYRUP
2

NOPE! I CAN SEE THE FOOD DIDN'T HELP! YOU'RE STILL HERE!
HOW ELSE CAN I MAKE A REPORT ON YOU AND YOUR FRIENDS?

HEY! WHO'S YOUR ITTY BITTY BUDDY?
Y-YOU SEE HIM?

WHY SHOULDN'T WE? HE'S RIGHT THERE!
WHO'S RIGHT THERE?

HIS NAME IS JINGLES! I THOUGHT HE WAS JUST A HAPPY HALLUCINATION!
WHO? WHO?

CLOSE IT, POP! YOU SOUND LIKE AN OWL!
ADULTS CAN'T SEE HIM!

WELL, WHAT'LL YOU HAVE RUNT?
DON'T WORRY ABOUT ME!
I'LL HELP MYSELF!
3

SNAP!
POP

EEP- AN ATOMIC SPECIAL!

WHO MADE THAT?
"JINGLES!"

I DON'T SEE ANY JINGLES! - I DON'T HEAR ANY JINGLES!
GULP! B-BUT SOMETHING IS EATING IT!

(GROAN) THAT'S PRETTY RICH AFTER A DIET OF REINDEER MILK!
YOU'D BETTER WALK IT OFF!
COLA

WALK? HAH! I'LL SHOW YOU HOW TO EXERCISE!

EEYIPE! W-WHAT WAS THAT?
ZOOM!
4

TSK-POP IS SURE SHOOK UP!
POP
CLOSED

WE'LL SEE YOU LATER!
SO LONG, JINGLES!
GLAD TO HAVE MET YOU!

I WANT YOU TO MEET MY GIRL, VERONICA!

LOVE TO, ARCHIE!
SNAP!

POW

HOW DID HE GET IN HERE!
HE DIDN'T EVEN RING!

HE DIDN'T EVEN OPEN THE DOOR, SIR!
5

WELL, IT'S THE YULETIDE SEASON! AND IT'S BETTER TO GIVE THAN RECEIVE!

-SO GIVE HIM THE OLD HEAVE HO, SMITHERS!

FOR ME, SIR! AND CHRISTMAS STILL A WEEK AWAY?

A-ONE, AND A-TWO, AND A ....
SNAP!

...T-THREE?

YOU'RE LOSING YOUR TOUCH, OLD MAN!
H-HE MUST BE STUDYING JUDO!
6

STRANGE THINGS ARE GOING ON HERE, SMITHERS!
I SUGGEST WE KEEP AN EYE ON HIM!

ALL RIGHT, ARCHIE! YOU MAY STAY!
BUT IF YOU STAY, YOU WORK!
W-WORK?

BRING IN THE TREE, SET IT UP AND DECORATE IT!

ULP! T-THAT'LL TAKE ALL AFTERNOON!

NOT WHEN YOU KNOW THE RIGHT PEOPLE!
SNAP!

-AND DON'T BREAK ANY... EEEEEEEE...
7

DADDY! WHAT'S WRONG? YOU LOOK **ILL**!
P-POSSIBLY B-BECAUSE I **AM** ILL!

WHY, ARCHIEKINS! WHO'S YOUR FRIEND?
THIS IS JINGLES! ONE OF MR. C'S BROWNIES!

WOO-WOO! SOMETIMES I **LOVE** MY WORK!

WHY, HE'S CUTE!
SHUCKS!

WHAT WOULD YOU LIKE FOR CHRISTMAS?
A TRIP TO THE MOON ON GOSSAMER WINGS?

ARCHIE!-WE'VE **GOT** TO SHOW HIM TO **BETTY**!
IT'S DONE!
SNAP!

P-PACK MY BAG, SMITHERS! I'M GOING ON A TRIP!
M-MAY I JOIN YOU, SIR?
POP
8

SAY! WHERE DID YOU THREE COME FROM?

...OR SHOULD I SAY, TWO AND A HALF!
(SIGH) -TO THINK THAT I HAVE TO LEAVE ALL THIS!

-BUT I'VE GOT TO MAKE MY REPORT TO THE MAN!

I'D LIKE TO SAY GOODBYE TO THE REST OF THE GANG!

TAKE US ALL TO MY HOUSE!
IT'S A SNAP!
SNAP!

FOR HE'S A JOLLY GOOD FELLOW, FOR HE'S A JOLLY GOOD FELLOW!
SNIFF!
9

JINGLES, BEFORE YOU GO, HERE'S A LITTLE SOMETHING TO REMEMBER ME BY!

I'M SURE YOU CAN CUT IT DOWN TO SIZE WITH NO TROUBLE!
Y-YOU'RE ALL HEART, ARCHIE!
SNAP!

(SNIFF)-PERFECT FIT! PERFECT GIFT!
YOU'LL ALL BE LISTED WITH THE GOOD ONES!

D-DO YOU THINK HE WAS REALLY HERE?
IF HE WASN'T, IT WAS AN AWFULLY NICE DREAM!
ZOOM!

HAH! DID YOU CATS EVER HAVE AN ATOMIC SPECIAL? DID YOU EVER OWN A KEEN SET OF THREADS LIKE THIS? MAN! YOU HAVEN'T LIVED!
(SIGH)- I LOSE MORE GOOD BROWNIES THAT WAY!
GOOD
INK
10

Jingles returns to help the gang with their Christmas spirit, but he's the one who needs help when he discovers Jangles is already on the scene! Can Jingles go from selfish to elfish before Christmas Eve?!

Archie in 'The Return of JINGLES'

IT'S THAT TIME OF YEAR AGAIN, OL' BUDDY!

I'M BACK TO SEE IF YOU CATS RATE THE REWARD THIS YULE!

-BUT MOSTLY I CAN'T WAIT TO SEE THE GANG!
C'MON!
POP

EEYIPE!
JINGLES! DON'T BE IN SUCH A HURRY!!

OOOPS! SORRY, ARCH!
SNAP

POP

WHEW! THAT'S BETTER!
2

JINGLES IT'S SO GOOD TO SEE YOU AGAIN! LET'S GO TELL BETTY THE GOOD NEWS!
WE'RE OFF!
SNAP

HI! WE'VE BEEN EXPECTING YOU!

JANGLES! WHAT ARE YOU DOING HERE? THIS IS MY ASSIGNMENT!

YOU BRAGGED ABOUT THESE KIDS SO MUCH LAST YEAR THAT I HAD TO COME SEE FOR MYSELF!

WELL, BLAST OFF, BUDDY! I'M WORKING THIS SIDE OF THE STREET!

WHY SHOULD YOU ALWAYS GET THE GOOD JOBS?
I'M STAYING!

HOW ABOUT A KNUCKLE SANDWICH FOR LUNCH, BIG MOUTH?
3

HEY, YOU MINIATURE DELINQUENTS! BROWNIES AREN'T SUPPOSED TO SCRAP!
R

LET'S LET JUGHEAD FIGURE IT OUT! HE'S A REGULAR KING SULLIVAN!
THAT'S SOLOMON, ARCHIE!

OKAY!
SNAP
SNAP

YOU LITTLE NUT! YOUR SNAP CANCELLED OUT MINE!

I'LL DO THE SNAPPING AROUND HERE!

HOW ABOUT SNAPPING A CLAMP ON THAT LIP OF YOURS?

WHY, YOU...
HEY! HOLD IT!
R
4

YOU'VE MET JUGHEAD, JINGLES!
YOU SNAP!
HMPH! BIG MAN!
SNAP!

HEY, JUG! LOOK WHO'S HERE!

YEAH! I HEARD YOU WERE COMING!
CHOMP!
CHOMP!

(CHOMP)-TOO BAD, BOYS! THIS IS THE LAST OF THE HAMBURGERS!
URP

JEEVES?
WHY, YOU WORMY LITTLE WART!

YOU'RE HEADIN' BACK TO THE POLE PRONTO!
SAYS WHO?
SAYS ME! AND THAT GOES FOR BOTH OF YOU!

SNAP!
SPLASH
SPLAT!
SNAP!
SPLOOSH!
SNAP!

T-THEY'RE MAKING THINGS APPEAR OUT OF N-NO WHERE!
PAILS OF WATER! EGGS! PIES!

(ULP)- T-THEY'RE GONE!
ALL OF THEM!
T-THEY MUST HAVE BEEN RECALLED!
POP
POP
POP

-A BLOT ON THE NAME OF SANTA CLAUS! A SIMPLE ASSIGNMENT! SEPARATE THE GOODS FROM THE BADS! THAT'S ALL I ASK! AND WHAT HAPPENS? A BRANNIGAN! A PIER SIX BRAWL! A RUNT SIZED RUMBLE!.... YOU OUGHT TO BE DRUMMED OUT OF THE BROWNIES' UNION! ETC...ETC...ETC......
Home Sweet Home
Merry Xmas
THE END

In a mischievous mood, Jingles makes a surprise appearance simply to work his magic... and wreak havoc... on Archie, Jughead and Reggie! Will the tables turn on this impish elf?

Archie in "SEASON OF MAGIC"

YIPES! A SNOWSTORM IN MY OWN BATHROOM MEANS ONE OF TWO THINGS! EITHER I'M OUT OF MY HEAD OR ***JINGLES*** IS BACK IN TOWN!

Doyle / White / Yoshida

BUSY! YOU KNOW THIS SEASON AT THE NORTH POLE! REALLY JUMPIN'! WORK, WORK, WORK! UGH!
RIVERSIDE

SO YOU CUT OUT TO COME DOWN AND VISIT YOUR OLD PALS!
BEATS WORKIN'!

BESIDES, I GET A KICK OUT OF DROPPING IN HERE AND SHOWING OFF MY MAGIC!

LIKE, FOR INSTANCE?
LIKE SO!

GAK! JINGLES! YOU PEACHY LITTLE PIPSQUEAK! YOU'RE BACK!
2

I KNOW THE WAY TO YOUR HEART IS THROUGH YOUR STOMACH!
DON'T TALK! EAT!

MMM! DELIGHTFUL! JUST DELIGHTFUL! WORDS CAN'T EXPRESS MY GRATITUDE!
JINGLES DOES WHAT HE ENJOYS DOING!
ZAP!

(GIGGLE) WHICH BRINGS US TO GOOD OL' ROTTEN REGGIE!

WATCH! INSTANT ICE PATCH!
ZAP!

EEEEEYOOOW!
ZOOM!
3

WHERE DID THAT ICE COME FROM?

A MINUTE AGO IT WASN'T THERE, AND SUDDENLY...

OUCH!
KLUNK!

THAT TREE WASN'T THERE, EITHER! NOW HOW... WHO... WHO... HOO HOO... HOOO...

JINGLES! COME OUT, YOU LITTLE SPELL-WEAVING SNAKE IN THE GRASS!
AH! HE REMEMBERS ME!
4

GO BACK! BACK ON YOUR OWN FROZEN TURF, YOU MISERABLE ELF!

SOME DAY YOUR BOSS WILL CATCH YOU GOOFING OFF AND *THEN* YOU'LL BE IN TROUBLE!
HAH!

OL' SANTA BABY IS MUCH TOO BUSY TO MISS A LITTLE DARLIN' LIKE ME!

OOPS!
I SPOKE TOO SOON!

EEK! *TWO* OF THEM!?
5

GAK! HALLUCINATIONS! I'M SEEING THINGS! MY GUILTY CONSCIENCE HAS CAUGHT UP WITH ME!

IT'S HOME AND A LONG BED REST FOR THIS SICK BROWNIE!
POOF!

WHA--HAPPENED?
HE'S GONE BACK TO THE NORTH POLE!
WELL, GOODY FOR US!

HA, HA! THAT LITTLE DING-A-LING DOESN'T REALIZE HOW MANY DEPARTMENT STORE SANTAS THERE ARE RUNNING AROUND IN THIS SEASON!
EMPLOYMENT AGENC
WANTED SANTA CLAUS TYPES
THE End.

Instead of a lump of coal for his stocking, Jingles gives Reggie an extra-meaningful Christmas present: a taste of his own medicine, pulling one practical joke after another on Riverdale's resident prankster!

HOWEVER, IF IT'S A MASTER WOODS-MAN YOU NEED, ALLOW ME TO OFFER MY SERVICES!
(SIGH)...I GUESS BEGGARS CAN'T BE CHOOSERS!
HOW DARE YOU CALL RIVERDALE'S MADCAP HEIRESS A BEGGAR?

OOH! HOW I'M GOING TO MANGLE THAT MANTLE IF I EVER GET UNWRAPPED!
SLAM!

YECH! WHAT A BIRDBRAIN I AM, TO LET HIM CATCH ME OFF GUARD THIS WAY!
IF MY FEET WERE LOOSE, I'D KICK MYSELF!

I'M READING THAT MIDGET MIND OF YOURS PAL! MY TINY TOE PACKS A TERRIFFIC WALLOP!
SHALL I DO THE JOB FOR YOU?
JINGLES!!
2

PLAYING HOOKEY FROM SANTA'S WORK-SHOP AGAIN, EH?
MORE LIKE A FORCED VACATION, ARCH!
ZAP

GOOFED ON TWELVE GROSS OF KEWPIE DOLLS!
PUT THEIR EYES IN THE BACK OF THEIR HEADS!
WHY DIDN'T YOU JUST CALL THEM "TEACHER" DOLLS?

BUT LET'S GET TO MY CAR! I'VE GOT TO GET TO THOSE WOODS ABOVE VERONICA'S HOUSE!

CAR?? WHERE I COME FROM, THOSE THINGS WENT OUT WITH THE BUGGY WHIP!
HANG ON!
ZAP
WHIRRRRRR

WHEW! THAT INSTANT TRAVEL TAKES YOUR BREATH AWAY!
WELL, WE BEAT YOUR FUNNY FRIEND TO THE SCENE!
3

OOH! HAVE I GOT A CHRISTMAS GIFT FOR *THAT* BIRD!
HOLD IT! LEAVE US NOT BE *CRUDE!*

SIT, LADIES! I'LL BRING YOU BACK A TREE THAT'LL MAKE YOUR EYES POP!
NEVER MIND POPPING OUR EYES, ...JUST SATISFY DADDY!

NOW THERE'S A SPECIMEN WORTHY OF MY TIME AND EFFORT!

DO SOMETHING, JINGLES! THAT TREE WILL PUT HIM *IN* AND ME *OUT!*
OH, I WOULDN'T SAY THAT!
ZAP

OH, JINGLES, THAT *IS* PRETTY!
HOW'S THIS GONNA LOOK IN YOUR LIVING ROOM ON CHRISTMAS MORN?
4

ARE YOU GOING TO HELP US OR ARE YOU GOING TO ACT THE FOOL ALL AFTERNOON ?

THERE'S THE AX AND THE STUMP!
I KNOW I CHOPPED DOWN A TREE!

MAYBE THE EXERTION MADE ME DIZZY AND I HAD HALLUCINATIONS!

WELL, I'LL TRY AGAIN! THIS LOOKS LIKE A NICE SPECIMEN!

GRUNT!
ZAP

CLANK
5

IT WAS A TREE! I SWEAR IT WAS A TREE!

...BUT NOW IT'S AN IRON POST!

...OH, NO!! THE WEEK BEFORE CHRISTMAS!... IT'S GOTTA BE!

OKAY, JINGLES, YOU MISERABLE LITTLE RUNT!... I KNOW YOU'RE HERE SOMEWHERE!

AW! YOU GUESSED!
ZAP
FLOOP
6

YOU HAUNTED LITTLE HORROR! I'LL CRUSH YOU LIKE THE PESKY LITTLE INSECT YOU ARE!

YOU'RE BARKING UP THE WRONG TREE, ROVER!
CRUNCH

REGGIE! YOU'RE WORSE THAN USELESS! SLEEPING IN THE SNOW WHEN YOU'RE SUPPOSED TO BE HELPING US!

COME ON, BETTY!... WE'LL GET OUT OF THESE WOODS AND FIND SOMEONE TO HELP US!
ER... WHICH WAY IS OUT?

(GROAN) I SEEM TO HAVE LOST MY BEARINGS!
HE DOESN'T EVEN KNOW WHICH WAY IS UP!
THEY CAN'T BE LOST IN THIS LITTLE PATCH OF WOODS!
EVERYTHING IS POSSIBLE WITH JINGLES ON THE JOB!
7

LOST! – LOST IN THIS IMPENETRABLE FOREST!
HELP! SOMEBODY SAVE ME! THE WORLD NEEDS MY GREATNESS!

ARCHIE!
AND JINGLES! WE'RE SAVED!

I GOT YOUR TREE FOR YOU!
SO WHAT! ... WE'RE STILL LOST!

STEP OVER HERE, STUPID!

THERE'S MY HOUSE! ARCHIE, YOU'RE MARVELOUS!!
IT WAS RIGHT IN FRONT OF YOUR NOSE, DUM, DUM!
8

THAT DOES IT! YOU TWO HAVE MADE A PATSY OUT OF ME FOR THE LAST TIME!

WOULD YOU BELIEVE, NEXT TO LAST?
WOK!

HE'S GOT MY TREE!
HE'S GOING TO DELIVER IT!

AIEEEEEEEEEE!
9

NOBODY WOULD BELIEVE IT CRASHED THROUGH THE WINDOW AND LANDED RIGHT IN THE STAND!

IT'LL BE A BEAUTIFUL TREE, ONCE WE GET THAT UGLY DECORATION OFF IT!

MAN, I'M INDEBTED TO YOU, JINGLES! HOW CAN I REPAY YOU?

KNOW ANYBODY WHO WANTS A KEWPIE DOLL WITH REAR VISION?

The End

The Archies prepare to spread a little holiday cheer by playing a "Toys For Tykes" benefit concert, but Reggie comes down with a nasty cold. In true Christmas spirit, however, Jingles The Elf agrees to fill in. There's only one problem—adults can't see him!

SCRIPT & PENCILS: BILL GOLLIHER INKS: RUDY LAPICK
COLORS: BARRY GROSSMAN LETTERS: BILL YOSHIDA

AW, SHUCKS!
WHAT'S HAPPENING AT THE NORTH POLE THESE DAYS?
WE'VE ALL BEEN WORKING AROUND THE CLOCK GETTING READY FOR SANTA'S BIG DAY!
SO I THOUGHT I'D TAKE A BREAK AND VISIT YOU GUYS!
WE'RE PRACTICING FOR A BENEFIT CONCERT TOMORROW NIGHT!
THAT SOUNDS LIKE FUN!
KOFF! KOFF!
REGGIE, ARE YOU GOING TO BE UP FOR THIS? YOUR COLD SOUNDS WORSE!

SANTA CLAUS IS COMIN' TO TOWN! SANTA CLAUS IS COMIN' TO TOWN!
GO FOR IT, JINGLES!
THAT WAS GREAT! WE NEVER KNEW YOU WERE A SINGER!
THEY DON'T CALL ME THE ELVIS ELF FOR NOTHING!
WHADDYA SAY, REGGIE, CAN I FILL IN FOR YOU?
WOW! THIS SHOULD BE SOME CHRISTMAS CONCERT COMPLETE WITH A REAL ELF!
AND THE BENEFIT IS RIGHT UP YOUR ALLEY! TOYS FOR TYKES!
USUALLY I'D MAKE A SNIDE REMARK, BUT THE WAY I FEEL, BE MY GUEST! KOFF
INSTEAD OF PAYING ADMISSION, PEOPLE BRING A TOY TO DONATE!
THEN THEY'RE DISTRIBUTED TO LESS FORTUNATE CHILDREN!
COOL!
DO YOU THINK SANTA WILL GIVE YOU A HARD TIME ABOUT TAKING OFF?
3

OH, KIDS?!
UH... HI, MOM!
I JUST WANTED TO TELL YOU THAT SOUNDED GREAT! YOU GUYS ARE IMPROVING!
THANKS!
HMPH!
SLAP!
I FORGOT ADULTS CAN'T SEE YOU!
YEAH! IT COMES IN HANDY SOMETIMES!
BUT THAT WON'T WORK IF YOU'RE SINGING LEAD FOR US!
ALL THE ADULTS WILL SEE IS AN EMPTY SPOT ON THE STAGE!
THEY CAN'T SEE YOU OR YOUR REGULAR OUTFIT!
BUT IF I MAKE A COSTUME AND DISGUISE FOR YOU TO WEAR, THEN EVERYONE SHOULD SEE THAT!
I'LL TAKE YOUR MEASUREMENTS AND GET TO WORK ON IT!
HEE! HEE! THAT TICKLES!
4

JINGLES! WHAT'S HAPPENING TO YOU?!
UH-OH! THE BIG GUY IS CALLING ME BACK!

BUT WHAT ABOUT THE CONCERT?!
DON'T WORRY! I'LL CONVINCE HIM TO GIVE ME THE TIME OFF!
POOF!

THE NEXT NIGHT...
IT'S ALMOST CONCERT TIME, AND NO JINGLES!
YEAH! AND REGGIE'S COLD IS WORSE! HE COULDN'T EVEN MAKE IT!
DRESSING ROOM

AND I GOT HIS LITTLE COSTUME ALL MADE SO HE'LL BE VISIBLE!
YOO-HOO! I'M HERE!
POOF!

IT'S JUST LIKE THE STAR TO SHOW UP AT THE LAST MINUTE!
HEY, COOL OUTFIT! NOW I'LL REALLY BE THE ELVIS ELF!
5

DID SANTA GIVE YOU A HARD TIME ?!
ACTUALLY, WHEN HE HEARD WHAT A GOOD CAUSE THIS WAS, HE INSISTED ON SENDING ALL THE OTHER ELVES FOR A REST AND RELAXATION BREAK!
AND SO...
WOW! CAN YOU BELIEVE ALL THESE TOYS?
I DON'T REMEMBER LETTING THAT MANY PEOPLE IN!
TOYS FOR TYKES
The Archies
TONIGHT!

BETTER WATCH OUT! BETTER NOT CRY! BETTER NOT POUT I'M TELLIN' YOU WHY...
THIS IS GREAT! THAT LITTLE GUY SINGING LEAD IS WONDERFUL!

YEAH! BUT I WONDER WHY THEY LEFT THE FIRST FEW ROWS EMPTY!
?

BUT, MOMMY, THEY NOT EMPTY!
WHAT AN IMAGINATION!
END

The Sugar Plum Fairy is one of Santa's most special sprites. Using her magical powers to spread Christmas cheer, she only appears to Riverdale's teens... Betty and Veronica in particular. While she may occasionally lose sight of her important mission, she always comes through with a happy, and often heartwarming ending.

SOME THINGS NEVER CHANGE
Betty & Veronica #156, 2001
by Kathleen Webb, Jeff Shultz and Henry Scarpelli

VISIONS OF A SUGAR PLUM
Betty & Veronica #108, 1997
by Kathleen Webb, Dan DeCarlo, Barry Grossman and Bill Yoshida

'TIS THE SEASON TO BE JOLLY
Betty & Veronica #120, 1998
by Kathleen Webb, Dan DeCarlo, Alison Flood, Barry Grossman and Bill Yoshida

SHE'S SO GIFTED
Veronica #191, 2009
by Dan Parent and Jim Amash

THE GIFTED
Betty & Veronica #169, 2002
by Kathleen Webb, Jeff Shultz, Henry Scarpelli, Bill Yoshida and Barry Grossman

The Sugar Plum Fairy pays her annual visit to Betty and Veronica, just in time to get everyone in the Christmas spirit... but can she possibly help the girls make Veronica's holiday party more festive?

Sugar Plum in "SOME THINGS NEVER CHANGE"

HEY! HI, GIRLS! IT'S YOUR OL' FRIEND, THE SUGAR PLUM FAIRY! MERRY CHRISTMAS!

YEAH!

SURE!

I HEAR YOU GIRLS HAVE BEEN HAVING SOME TROUBLE GETTING INTO THE HOLIDAY SPIRIT! SO I'LL TRY AGAIN... *MERRY CHRISTMAS!*

SCRIPT: KATHLEEN WEBB
PENCILS: JEFF SCHULTZ
INKS: HENRY SCARPELLI

THIS LOOKS LIKE A JOB FOR... THE SUGAR PLUM FAIRY!

AFTER ALL, AS ONE OF SANTA'S HELPERS, IT'S MY JOB TO ASSIST PEOPLE IN FINDING THEIR CHRISTMAS SPIRIT!

AND YOU TWO LOOK LIKE YOU COULD USE A LOT OF HELP!
AREN'T YOU OBSERVANT?
IT'S THIS PARTY!

I SEE PEOPLE HAVING A GREAT TIME! IT'S ALL VERY MERRY!
IT'S ALL WRONG!

THIS IS THE HAPPIEST, MOST FESTIVE TIME OF THE YEAR! 'TIS THE SEASON TO BE JOLLY!
SO ALL THE SONGS TELL US!

WOULD YOU LIKE IT BETTER IF EVERYONE WAS ALL GLOOM AND DOOM?
NO, THAT'S NOT IT!
2

THIS PARTY ISN'T ANY DIFFERENT FROM ALL THE OTHER PARTIES RON'S GIVEN THIS YEAR!
AND THAT'S THE TROUBLE!
IT DOESN'T FEEL LIKE CHRISTMAS SOMEHOW!
EXCEPT FOR THE MISTLETOE GETTING ITS ANNUAL WORKOUT...

YOU'D NEVER KNOW THIS WAS A CHRISTMAS PARTY!
SO HOW DO WE MAKE IT MORE CHRISTMASSY?

FOR STARTERS, GET RID OF ALL THIS FUSSY NOUVEAU CUISINE, AND REPLACE IT WITH CHRISTMAS COOKIES, HOT CHOCOLATE AND CIDER!
POP!

BLAZE UP THE YULE LOG IN THE FIREPLACE...

AND TURN OFF THE RAP, HIP HOP AND ROCK FOR THE EVENING!
BUT, WHAT'LL WE DO FOR MUSIC?
STRANGE SILENCE!
ZAP!
3

GATHER 'ROUND THE PIANO AND MAKE YOUR OWN MUSIC!
YOU MEAN... SING CHRISTMAS CAROLS?!

HOW HORRIBLY OLD-FASHIONED... OUT-DATED... OUT-MODED...
AND DELIGHTFULLY TRADITIONAL!
PLAY!!

DECK THE HALLS WITH BOUGHS OF HOLLY...

HEY, WE SOUND PRETTY GOOD!
WE OUGHTA BE ON THE ROAD!
HOW ABOUT IT, RON?

YOU MEAN... GO CAROLLING?... NOW?
NOW IS BETTER THAN NEVER!

OKAY, BUT... EVERYBODY HAS TO COME BACK TO MY HOUSE WHEN WE FINISH!
YOU BET! WE'RE GONNA NEED THAT FIRE AND HOT CHOCOLATE!
4

WE WISH YOU A MERRY CHRISTMAS... AND A HAPPY NEW YEAR!

LATER, BACK AT RON'S...
THAT WAS SO MUCH FUN, RON!
NOT LIKE YOUR USUAL PARTIES AT ALL!

NOW I'M REALLY IN A CHRISTMAS MOOD!
LET'S DO THIS EVERY YEAR!
D-UH-H... YEAH!

WHAT'D I TELL YOU, HUH? HUH?
THERE'S SOMETHING TO BE SAID FOR TRADITION, I GUESS!

THE MORE THINGS CHANGE, THE MORE WE RELY ON THINGS THAT NEVER CHANGE!!
LIKE GOOD FRIENDS LIKE YOU!
END

The Sugar Plum Fairy comes to Betty and Veronica for help when she has... what else?... man trouble! It's up to Betty and Veronica to make sure she has a Merry Christmas after all!

Betty and Veronica

IN "VISIONS OF A SUGAR PLUM" PART ONE

RON... VERONICA ... TELL ME I'M NOT GOING CRAZY...TELL ME YOU HEAR THAT TREE CRYING!

HUH ?!? WH-YOU'RE RIGHT! IT IS MAKING A SOBBING SOUND!

SNIFF!

SOB!

BUT SUGAR PLUM, YOUR JOB IS TO HELP PEOPLE FIND THEIR CHRISTMAS SPIRIT!
HOW CAN YOU LOSE YOURS?
(SIGH) MAN TROUBLE!

A SMALL FRY LIKE YOU HAS GUY TROUBLE?
QUIET, RON! TELL US ABOUT IT, SUGAR PLUM!

WELL... HIS NAME IS TROLL!
HE'S QUITE A HUNK OF AN ELF! HE LOADS SANTA'S SLEIGH EVERY CHRISTMAS EVE!

WE'VE BEEN DATING SINCE THIS SUMMER ...AND I THOUGHT FOR SURE HE'D ASK ME TO THE UPCOMING NEW YEAR'S EVE BASH AT THE NORTH POLE!

...BUT HE HASN'T YET, AND I JUST KNOW HE'S GOING TO ASK SOME-ONE ELSE!
SOUNDS LIKE THE WAY ARCHIE TREATS ME!

HAVE YOU GOT A RIVAL TOO?
OH, YEAH... AND SHE'S EVERY BIT AS LOVEABLE AS YOURS!
HEY!
2

I WOULDN'T BE TOO QUICK TO THROW INSULTS AT SOMEONE WHO COULD HELP YOU OUT!
HOW? H-HOW?

FIRST, LET'S SEE IF YOU CAN ENLARGE YOURSELF TO **OUR** SIZE!
OH, SURE! THAT'S EASY!

SEE? I JUST LOSE THE WINGS AND THE ANTENNAE!
POOF!
GOOD!
WHAT'S THIS ALL ABOUT, RON?

WE'RE GOING SHOPPING FOR A NEW OUTFIT THAT'LL KNOCK YOUR ELF'S EYES OUT!
HE WON'T SEE YOUR RIVAL FOR DUST!

MEANWHILE, IN THE FROZEN REGIONS OF THE NORTH POLE...

IS THAT (GULP) REALLY SUGAR PLUM ?!?
WHAT DO YOU THINK OF THIS DRESS, GIRLS ?

OH, THAT'S GORGEOUS! DON'T YOU THINK, RON ?
IT'S PERFECT! HE OUGHT TO LOVE YOU IN THAT !
HE ALREADY DOES!

IN FACT, WHY DON'T I JUST--
HEY, RALPHIE, LOOK!
MUST BE SOME NEW ROBOT TOY!

C'MON! LET'S CATCH HIM! WE'LL TAKE HIM APART TO SEE HOW IT WORKS!
YIPE!!

I'LL CATCH UP TO SUGAR PLUM LATER! FIRST I'VE GOT TO OUTRUN THESE LITTLE CREEPS!
THERE HE GOES!
ZZZZZ
ZOOOOM!

ALL THAT SHOPPING HAS MADE ME THIRSTY! WHAT SAY WE TROT OVER TO POP TATE'S FOR A SODA ?
SOUNDS GOOD TO ME!
5

HEY, ARCH! LOOKA THAT!!!
WOW!!!

HI THERE! HAVEN'T WE MET SOMEWHERE BEFORE?
WHY, YES! NOW THAT YOU MENTION IT!
DO TELL!

WEELL... AT LEAST SHE'S GOT HER CHRISTMAS SPIRIT BACK!
YEAH... AT THE EXPENSE OF OURS!
TEE HEE! GIGGLE!

JUST AT THAT MOMENT...
(WHEW) I FINALLY MANAGED TO SHAKE THOSE KIDS!
SEEMS TO ME I HEARD THE GIRLS SAY THEY WERE HEADED HERE!
POP TAT

THERE THEY ARE! B-BUT... WHAT'S THIS? ARE THOSE CREEPS BOTHERING HER?
I'LL PUT A STOP TO THAT!
PO

FZAD!
REGGIE? ARCHIE? W-WHAT'S WRONG?
TO BE CONTINUED-6

"VISIONS OF A SUGAR PLUM"

PART TWO

ARCHIE? REGGIE? SPEAK TO ME, GUYS! BETTY, VERONICA! W-WHAT'S WRONG WITH THEM?

THEY ACT LIKE THEY'RE UNDER SOME SORT OF SPELL!

GASP!

THAT'S RIGHT! THEY *ARE*!!

SO YOU GOT ALL THOSE MUSCLES LOADING SANTA'S SLEIGH, HMM?
WELL... ...ER... GEE... YEAH!
MMM! YOU MUST LIFT ALL THE HEAVY STUFF!

THAT DOES IT!!!
ZAP!

TWO CAN PLAY THE FREEZE GAME!
WHAT'D YA DO *THAT* FOR?

YOU LOOKED LIKE YOU WERE ENJOYING THAT JUST A LITTLE TOO MUCH!
WELL, *YOU* DIDN'T LOOK TOO UNHAPPY EITHER!

TROLLIE, HONEY, I GOT ALL DOLLED UP JUST FOR YOU!
I'D LOVE TO HEAR WHAT YOU HAVE TO SAY!
R-REALLY?

WOULD... WOULD YOU LIKE TO GO WITH ME TO THE BIG NEW YEAR'S BASH AT THE NORTH POLE?
I THOUGHT YOU WERE GOING TO TAKE SOMEONE ELSE...

...LIKE MY RIVAL GARLAND!
NOW YOU KNOW THERE'S NO ONE ELSE I'D RATHER TAKE THAN YOU!

SO HOW ABOUT IT?
(SIGH) YES! THERE'S NO ONE I'D RATHER GO WITH!
BETTY? VERONICA?

I GOTTA STOP PUTTING SO MUCH ICE IN THE SOFT DRINKS, I GUESS!
WHOOPS! WE FORGOT ABOUT THE KIDS!
YIPES!

FZAD!
9

(WHEW) THANKS! I WAS GETTING STIFF HOLDING THAT POSITION!
ARE YOU GUYS ALL MADE UP NOW ?
? ? ?
YES! AND I OWE IT ALL TO YOU TWO! THANKS TO YOU...
... I HAVE MY DATE AND MY CHRISTMAS SPIRIT BACK!
NOW IT'S TIME FOR US TO HEAD BACK TO THE NORTH POLE!
SEE YA!
POOF!
'BYE!
UMM ... SAY... ARCHIE... WHO ARE YOU TAKING TO THE NEW YEAR'S EVE DANCE AT SCHOOL ?
ER... WELL ... UM ... AH ...
HE'S TAKING ME, AREN'T YOU, ARCHIEKINS?
HE DOESN'T NEED YOUR HELP TO MAKE UP HIS MIND, VERONICA!
AND I SUPPOSE YOU WEREN'T GOING TO HELP HIM OUT A BIT ??
10

HEY! MAYBE I'D LIKE TO TAKE SOMEONE ELSE FOR A CHANGE!
WHAT?!

ER... I THINK IT'S TIME FOR US TO TAKE OUR LEAVE!
NOPE! THIS KINDA STUFF IS WHERE MY JOB COMES IN!

HOLD IT!!!

C'MON, KIDS! 'TIS THE SEASON! WHERE'S YOUR CHRISTMAS SPIRIT, HMMM-?

SHE'S RIGHT! LET'S JUST SAY WE'LL ALL GO TO THE DANCE TOGETHER!
SUITS ME!
WHEW
YOU'VE DONE YOUR JOB AGAIN, SUGAR PLUM! MERRY CHRISTMAS!
AND A MERRY CHRISTMAS IT WILL BE, TOO!
AND A HAPPY NEW YEAR!
The END

The Sugar Plum Fairy helps Veronica shake her cold so Veronica can shake it on the dance floor at the annual Christmas dance!

WHAT ARE YOU DOING OUT OF BED STANDING IN A DRAFTY DOORWAY?
WAIDING FOR YOU TO COME INZIDE AN' CLOSE THE DOOR!

(SNORT) DADDY DINKS I SHOULD BE UP IN BED, TOO!
CONSIDERING YOU SOUND LIKE A CEMENT MIXER...

...SHOULDN'T YOU BE?
IT'S CHRISBUS, BEDDIE! I DON' WAN' TO BE IN BED!

I WAN' TO BE OUD DERE, CELEBRADING! I DON' LIKE BEING COOBED UB IN HERE WID A ⁝ WHEEZE ⁝ ⁝ SNORT ⁝ ⁝ COUGH ⁝ STUBID COLD!
WHO WOULD?

SOUNDS LIKE YOU'RE GONNA MISS THE BIG CHRISTMAS DANCE AT THE SCHOOL TONIGHT!
IF I DON' GED ANY BEDDER BY TONIGHT, I *WILL*!

(SIGH) AND WID THE WAY I FEEL... (COUGH) DERE'S NOT BUCH CHANCE OF MY GEDDING BEDDER!
WHO SAYS?
2

YOU MEAN... YOU CAN MAKE HER BETTER?
NOT ME! I DON'T HAVE THE CURE FOR THE COMMON COLD!

HOWEVER... SANTA DRINKS A SPECIAL HERBAL TEA WHENEVER HE GETS THE SNIFFLES AT CHRISTMAS!
MRS. CLAUS BREWS IT OUT OF THE ESSENCE OF CHRISTMAS CHEER!

IT SEEMS TO WORK WONDERS FOR HIM! WANT ME TO BRING YOU SOME?
WOULD YOU? I'D LOVE-UH-LUH-AH-AH-CHOOO!!

I'LL ASSUME THAT MEANS "YES!" MEET YOU IN THE LODGE KITCHEN IN TEN MINUTES!
WE'LL BE THERE!
YOU BET!
POOF!

LET'S SEE NOW... MRS. CLAUS KEEPS THE TEA HERE IN THE NORTH POLE PANTRY...
AH! THERE IT IS! IN THAT CANISTER!
ESSENCE OF CHRISTMAS CHEER JAR
FRUIT CAKE
CANDY CANES
POOF
ASSORTED CANDIES

HERE YOU ARE, BETTY! I HOPE YOU HAVE THE HOT WATER BOILING!
I USED THE MICROWAVE TO HEAT THE WATER! HOW MUCH TEA SHOULD WE USE?
POP!
3

HMM? SANTA'S KIND OF A BIG GUY! I DON'T THINK SHE'LL NEED MUCH, THOUGH!
I'LL BREW JUST A TEASPOONFUL, THEN! HERE, RON!

HOW'S IT TASTE?
MMM... LIKE FRUITCAKE, GINGERBREAD, PEPPERMINT AND EGGNOG, ALL AT ONCE!

HOW DO YOU FEEL?
GREAT!!!

THANKS, SUGAR PLUM! NOW I CAN GO TO THE DANCE TONIGHT!
IN FACT, I'M GOING UPSTAIRS RIGHT NOW TO START GETTING READY!
WHAT'S WRONG?

I'M JUST WONDERING... THIS STUFF IS FOR SANTA AFTER ALL...I HOPE THERE AREN'T ANY SIDE EFFECTS!
SIDE EFFECTS? FROM THE ESSENCE OF CHRISTMAS CHEER?

WHAT KIND OF SIDE EFFECTS COULD COME FROM SOMETHING AS INNOCENT AS--
HO HO HO!
4

HO-HO-HO! MY DANCE DRESS ISN'T SUITABLE FOR THE SEASON!
I THINK SOME-THING RED AND WHITE MIGHT BE HO-HO-JOLLY!
THIS MUST BE YOUR SIDE EFFECT! HOW LONG DO YOU THINK IT'LL LAST?
I-I'M NOT SURE! I'D BETTER GO ASK MRS. CLAUS!
POOF!
MANY HO-HO'S LATER...
HEY, BETTY! MRS. CLAUS SAID THE TEA'S EFFECTS SHOULD WEAR OFF AFTER MIDNIGHT!
UH-HUH! YEAH! BIG DEAL!
POOF!

WHAT'S WRONG? I THOUGHT YOU'D BE MORE POPULAR AT THE DANCE WITH RON HO-HO'ING ALL OVER!
AH, BUT THIS IS VERONICA LODGE PLAYING SANTA CLAUS, NOT KRIS KRINGLE!

HO-HO-HO! AND WHAT WOULD YOU LIKE FOR CHRISTMAS, LITTLE MAN!
HOW ABOUT A NICE, BIG SMOOCH?
HEY! IT'S MY TURN TO SIT ON SANTA'S LAP!
I THINK THIS IS DEFINITELY A CASE OF THE CURE BEING WORSE THAN THE ILLNESS!
END

Encouraged by her parents to give homemade gifts from the heart this holiday season, Veronica is at a loss... until the Sugar Plum Fairy helps her discover her true talent!

Veronica in SHE'S SO GIFTED

I WANT TO SHOW YOU SOME-THING!
BUT KEEP IT QUIET!
LET ME GUESS! IS IT MOM'S CHRISTMAS PRESENT?!
YES!

WHERE IS IT?
RIGHT HERE!

I'M PAINTING HER A PICTURE!
WHY WOULD YOU WANT TO DO THAT?

WHY NOT HIRE A PROFESSIONAL ARTIST TO DO ONE?
I WANT TO DO SOMETHING PERSONAL THIS CHRISTMAS!

YOUR MOTHER AND I ARE GOING TO MAKE EACH OTHER'S GIFTS THIS YEAR!
2

D-DID WE LOSE OUR FORTUNE?!
NO! WE JUST WANT TO DO SOMETHING MORE MEANINGFUL THIS YEAR!

UH-OH! DOES THAT MEAN I'M GETTING A PAPER MACHÉ KNICK KNACK FOR CHRISTMAS?

DON'T WORRY! WE'LL RESORT TO CRASS COMMERCIALIZATION FOR YOU, HONEY!
WHEW! THAT'S A RELIEF!

WHAT ARE YOU WORKING ON, MOM?

I'M MAKING THIS FRAME FOR YOUR FATHER TO KEEP IN HIS OFFICE!
I'LL PUT A PHOTO OF OUR FAMILY IN IT!

VERY NICE! THE MALL AWAITS!
'BYE, NOW!
3

POOF
VERONICA! I'M ASHAMED OF YOU!
SUGAR PLUM FAIRY!
I GUESS IT'S TIME FOR MY ANNUAL BROW BEATING!
YOUR PARENTS ARE ENJOYING THE TRUE MEANING OF THE HOLIDAY SEASON!
YOU COULD LEARN A THING OR TWO FROM THEM!
LISTEN! I KNOW THE TRUE MEANING-- I JUST LIKE PRESENTS, TOO!
WOULDN'T IT BE NICE TO GIVE FROM THE HEART THIS YEAR?
I'LL THINK ABOUT IT!
I'M STOPPING TO PICK UP BETTY!
AH--! GOOD OL' BETTY!
4

OH, I KNOW! SHE'S PERFECT!
SPARE ME THE COMPARISONS!

HI, BETTY! ARE YOU READY?
ALMOST! I'M JUST WRAPPING THIS GIFT!

IT'S NOT LOOKING TOO GOOD!
HERE, LET ME HAVE AT IT!

THAT'S NICE OF YOU, VERONICA!
SUGAR PLUM! NICE TO SEE YOU!

HOW'S MY FAVORITE SPREADER OF HOLIDAY CHEER?
GREAT!
THERE! HOW'S THIS?
WOW!!
5

THAT'S GORGEOUS! SUGAR PLUM, DID YOU USE YOUR MAGIC?

ABSOLUTELY NOT! I DID THIS!
YOU TURNED IT INTO A WORK OF ART!

I HAVE BOUGHT A FEW HUNDRED THOUSAND GIFTS IN MY LIFE!
I'VE HAD PLENTY OF PRACTICE!

THAT'S IT, VERONICA!
THAT'S YOUR GIFT!!

NO... THIS IS BETTY'S GIFT!
NO! I MEAN YOUR GIFT, AS IN "GIFTED"!
USE YOUR GIFT TO SPREAD HOLIDAY CHEER!
6

YOU MEAN I SHOULD WRAP MY FRIENDS' AND FAMILY'S GIFTS FOR THEM?
EXACTLY!
WOW! I DO LOVE TO WRAP!
I'LL DO IT! FREE GIFT WRAPPING FOR EVERYONE!

I'LL CALL AND E-MAIL EVERYONE AND TELL THEM TO BRING THEIR GIFTS OVER!
THE GIFT OF GIFTS! WHAT A WONDERFUL IDEA!

SO...
THIS IS FOR MY MOM!
THIS IS FOR MY DAD!

AND THIS IS FOR BETTY!
YOU WILL WRAP THAT ONE FOR ME, TOO, RIGHT?

OF COURSE!
JUST REMEMBER TO BUY ME SOMETHING BETTER THAN THIS!
7

AND SO!
HERE YOU GO, RON! THIS'S ACTUALLY QUITE NICE OF YOU...
I GUESS IT MUST BE A CHRISTMAS MIRACLE!

DON'T PUSH IT!

HERE YOU GO!
THANKS, RON!
YOU'RE THE BEST, RON!
THIS IS A VERY WONDERFUL THING YOU'RE DOING, RON!

SO...
I MUST ADMIT, THESE ARE WORKS OF ART!
POOF
NICE JOB, VERONICA!

THANKS! BUT I'M OUT OF NAME TAGS!
I HAVE TO FIND SOME MORE!
8

Whew! HERE'S SOME IN THIS DRAWER!
THANK GOODNESS! THIS SAVES ME A TRIP OUTSIDE!

A FEW DAYS LATER...
WHAT A NICE THING YOU'RE DOING, DEAR!
I'M PROUD OF YOUR GIVING SPIRIT!

THANKS! I'M ALL FINISHED!
I HAVE TO CALL EVERYONE TO PICK UP THEIR PRESENTS!

WHAT'S THAT ALL OVER THE FLOOR?
HMM... LOOKS LIKE GIFT TAGS!

WHAT?! THESE ARE THE TAGS OFF OF ALL THE GIFTS I WRAPPED! THEY FELL OFF! HOW?!

I GOT THEM FROM THE HALL DRAWER!
THOSE ARE YEARS OLD! THEY MUST'VE LOST ALL THEIR STICKINESS!
9

MOM!
WITHOUT TAGS, HOW WILL I KNOW WHAT BELONGS TO WHO?!!
BAWL!
THE ONLY THING TO DO IS UNWRAP EVERYTHING AND REDO IT!!

SOB!
I'LL BE UP ALL NIGHT!!

I'LL HELP YOU, DEAR!
AND SO WILL I!

The NEXT MORNING...
SNORE
ZZZ
ZZ
Z
EXCUSE ME, BUT PEOPLE ARE HERE TO PICK UP THEIR PRESENTS!
10

THEY'RE BEAUTIFUL!
YOU'VE OUTDONE YOURSELF!
THANKS, VERONICA!
MERRY CHRISTMAS!
LATER...
THAT'S THE LAST OF THE GIFTS!
THANK YOU SO MUCH FOR HELP!
LET'S EXCHANGE OUR GIFTS NOW!
NO NEED! YOU BOTH GAVE ME THE BEST GIFT OF ALL!
THEN I GUESS YOU WON'T WANT THAT BRAND NEW WARDROBE WE BOUGHT YOU!
WELL! LET'S NOT BE TOO HASTY!!
AND... THAT'S A WRAP!
END

The Sugar Plum Fairy is sent on her most important holiday mission yet: to show Betty and Veronica that friendship is the greatest gift of all!

Betty and Veronica in "The Gifted"

SUGAR PLUM, I'VE RECEIVED REPORTS ON BETTY COOPER AND VERONICA LODGE THAT ARE RATHER DISTRESSING!

HOW SO, BOSS?

I'LL STOP HERE AT BETTY'S, FIRST!
FALALALA LAAA... HMM... HMM... HMM... HMM...
POOF!
GLUE

HI, CHEERFUL! WHAT'RE YOU UP TO?
OH, HI, SUGAR PLUM FAIRY!

I'M PUTTING THE FINISHING TOUCHES ON VERONICA'S CHRISTMAS GIFT!
WHAT IS IT?

AN EMBELLISHED PHOTO ALBUM FILLED WITH MY FAVORITE PHOTOS OF VERONICA AND ME!
SOME OF THE PHOTOS GO WAAAY BACK!

HOW SWEET! THE BEST KIND OF A CHRISTMAS PRESENT IS A HOME-MADE ONE! THEY'RE FULL OF SUCH LOVE!
(SIGH) I GUESS SO!

THE TROUBLE IS, EVERY YEAR VERONICA GOES OUT OF HER WAY TO BUY ME A GORGEOUS, EXPENSIVE CHRISTMAS PRESENT!
2

AND EVERY YEAR I GIVE HER A CHEAP, HOMEMADE GIFT! I CAN'T AFFORD ANYTHING FANCY!
GLUE
WOULD YOU BUY HER SOMETHING THAT COST A LOT IF YOU COULD?
MAYBE!
BUT I ALWAYS MAKE HER GIFTS, BECAUSE THAT WAY THEY SEEM MORE PERSONAL!
DO YOU LIKE THE GIFTS VERONICA GIVES YOU?
OH, YES! THEY'RE ALWAYS SOMETHING I'D LOVE TO BUY FOR MYSELF! SHE HAS THE KNACK OF FINDING THE PERFECT GIFT!
(SIGH) THAT'S WHY I FEEL BAD ABOUT GIVING HER SOMETHING SO CHEAP BY COMPARISON!
ER... I'LL BE RIGHT BACK, BETTY!
Y'KNOW, I'VE GOT A HUNCH ABOUT ALL THIS!
TO CONFIRM IT, I'LL CHECK ON VERONICA!
3

AND WHERE ELSE WOULD SHE BE, BUT AT THE MALL?
HI, WEALTHY ONE!
POP!
(SIGH) OH, HELLO, SUGAR PLUM!

DON'T SOUND SO THRILLED TO SEE ME!
(BIGGER SIGH!) I'VE GOT A REAL PROBLEM ON MY HANDS!

I'VE JUST FOUND THE PERFECT GIFT FOR BETTY...
... BUT IT'LL BE NOTHING COMPARED TO WHAT SHE'LL GIVE ME!

BETTY ALWAYS MAKES THESE ABSOLUTELY WONDERFUL HAND-MADE GIFTS! THINGS SHE PUTS HOURS AND HOURS INTO!

DO YOU LIKE THE HANDMADE GIFTS BETTY GIVES YOU?
YES... (SNIFF) I'VE KEPT EVERY ONE! I KNOW THEY COME FROM HER HEART!
LIMIT 5 ITEMS
OKAY... HERE'S WHAT YOU OUGHT TO DO WHEN YOU GIVE HER YOUR GIFT... BZZ... BZZ...
DO YOU THINK I SHOULD...?
BETTY! I'VE GOT THE PERFECT SOLUTION TO YOUR PROBLEM!
YOU'VE GOT TO BZZZ... BZZZ...
WILL THAT REALLY WORK!?
POP!
COME THE BIG DAY OF EXCHANGING GIFTS...
BEFORE I GIVE THIS TO YOU, BETTY, I HAVE A CONFESSION TO MAKE!
YOU, TOO? YOU FIRST!
EVERY YEAR I'M ALWAYS AFRAID YOU'LL THINK MY GIFT IS FLASHY AND IMPERSONAL!
BUT I DON'T FEEL THAT WAY!
I ALWAYS THINK YOU'LL FEEL MY GIFT IS TOO CHINTZY!
I'D NEVER THINK THAT ABOUT SOME-THING YOU'VE MADE!
5

AND I KNOW YOU PUT A LOT OF LOVE INTO WHAT YOU BUY ME!
WE'VE BOTH BEEN A COUPLE OF GOOFS!

THAT'S WHY I TOLD YOU TO TELL EACH OTHER THE TRUTH!
POP!
SUGAR PLUM!

IT'S TIME YOU STOPPED WORRYING ABOUT HOW YOU FEEL, AND THOUGHT MORE ABOUT THE OTHER PERSON!

AFTER ALL ... YOUR GIFTS CERTAINLY SHOW HOW MUCH YOU CARE ABOUT EACH OTHER!

(SNIFF) OH, RON, THE GIFT OF YOUR FRIENDSHIP IS THE BEST PRESENT I'VE EVER RECEIVED!
(SOB) I FEEL EXACTLY THE SAME WAY ABOUT, YOU, DEAR FRIEND!
THEY'VE JUST GIVEN ME A VERY SPECIAL CHRISTMAS GIFT!
END

If you think it's fun when either the Jingles the Elf or the Sugar Plum Fairy visit Riverdale's teens, just wait until you see the comedic chaos that ensues when the pair team up! Yes, there's a whole batch of Christmas magic in the air... along with a bit of mischief, competition and maybe even some love! Those whimsical sprites know how to liven up every yuletide season!

HOLIDAY WATCH
***Betty & Veronica #244*, 2009**
by Dan Parent, Jeff Shultz, Rich Koslowski, Jack Morelli and Barry Grossman

JINGLES ALL THE WAY
***Betty & Veronica Spectacular #86,* 2009**
by Dan Parent, Rich Koslowski, Rosario "Tito" Peña and Jack Morelli

THE NAUGHTY CLAUSE
***Archie #639*, 2013**
by Alex Segura, Gisele, Rich Koslowski, Digikore Studios and Jack Morelli

It just wouldn't be the holidays without a visit from Jingles the Elf and the Sugar Plum Fairy, but now that they're love-struck they need someone to make sure they don't slack on their duties... and Santa has assigned that task to Betty and Veronica!

Betty and Veronica® in HOLIDAY WATCH

SCRIPT: DAN PARENT PENCILS: JEFF SHULTZ INKING: RICH KOSLOWSKI LETTERING: JACK MORELLI COLORING: BARRY GROSSMAN

POOF
SPEAKING OF HOLIDAY TRADITIONS!

SUGAR PLUM!
IT'S GOOD TO SEE YOU AGAIN!

I GUESS DOING YOUR ANNUAL HOLIDAY CHECK-UP ON US!
I HAVE TO SEE HOW MY GIRLS ARE DOING!

AFTER ALL, I'VE GOT TO REPORT TO THE BIG GUY IN RED AT THE NORTH POLE!

WHY DON'T YOU LEAVE THAT TO ME?
POOF

JINGLES! WOW! WE'RE HAVING A REAL HOLIDAY PARTY HERE!
2

HI, JINGLES! HOW HAVE YOU BEEN?
NOT TOO BAD, SUGAR PLUM!

WOW! YOU TWO ARE USUALLY AT EACH OTHER'S THROATS! WHAT'S GOING ON?
NOTHING AT ALL!

WINK
giggle!

WANNA GRAB A HOT COCOA?
SURE! BYE, GIRLS!
MERRY CHRISTMAS
3

JINGLES AND SUGAR PLUM ARE MY HOLIDAY WATCHDOGS! THEY WATCH OVER THINGS FOR ME!

4

THEY'VE BEEN SO DISTRACTED, I NEED SOMEONE TO WATCH OVER THEM!
AND I THINK I KNOW WHO TO CHOOSE!

LATER...
ARE THERE ANY CHRISTMAS SHOWS ON?
KLIK
WELL, THERE'S SANTA CLAUS!

HELLO, BETTY AND VERONICA! I NEED YOUR HELP!
WOW! IS THIS SOME SORT OF INTERACTIVE SHOW?

THIS IS THE REAL SANTA CLAUS! I'M USING YOUR TELE-VISION TO TALK TO YOU!

WOW! HOW CAN WE HELP YOU, SANTA?
I NEED YOU TO WATCH OVER JINGLES AND SUGAR PLUM!

THEY'RE TOO DISTRACTED WITH EACH OTHER!
SO WE NOTICED!
5

BUT HOW WILL WE WATCH THEM?
THEY'LL BE TAKING ON HUMAN FORM TO WATCH OVER YOU!

REMEMBER JIMMY? AND SUMMER?
YES! SO THEY'RE REALLY JINGLES AND SUGAR PLUM?

RIGHT! BUT YOU HAVE TO KEEP THAT A SECRET BETWEEN US!
ALL OF RIVERDALE KNOWING THAT WOULD CAUSE TOO MUCH OF A DISTRACTION!

WEAR THOSE BROACHES! I'LL BE ABLE TO MONITOR EVERYTHING THROUGH THEM!
SURE THING, SANTA!

AND I'LL MAKE SURE YOU GIRLS STAY OFF THE NAUGHTY LIST FOR ALL YOUR HELP! UH, LET ME CORRECT MYSELF!

I'LL MAKE SURE VERONICA STAYS OFF THE NAUGHTY LIST!
hmph!
6

LATER, AT POP'S...
HI, GIRLS! I'M BACK!
WOW! IT'S JIMMY! HOW CONVENIENT!

WHAT DO YOU MEAN?
IT'S JUST ODD HOW YOU ALWAYS SHOW UP AT CHRISTMAS!

WELL, MY FAMILY IS VISITING RELATIVES IN TOWN!
IF YOU SAY SO...

hmm! IS THAT WHO I THINK IT IS?
YES, IT'S...

SUMMER!
WOW! ANOTHER COINCIDENCE!

MAY I HAVE THIS SEAT?
WELL, I'M AFRAID IT'S TAKEN...
7

I'M MEETING ARCHIE HERE!
SORRY, JIMMY!

WE HAVE TO KEEP OUR COVER, REMEMBER?
OKAY, OKAY!

I'LL SIT WITH THESE TWO LOVELIES!
LUCKY US!
POP'S

SOON...
HE'S WATCHING HER LIKE A HAWK!
GRRR...

ZAP
SPIN!
WHAT?! HOW DID THAT HAPPEN?!
8

I WONDER! TIME TO COOL OFF, JIMMY!
ZAP

FLOP
DID YOU SEE THAT?! THAT SUNDAE JUST FLEW THROUGH THE AIR!

THESE TWO ARE IN DANGER OF EXPOSING THEMSELVES!

LATER...
THERE'S SUMMER-- ER, SUGAR PLUM!
MAYBE IF WE HANG OUT WITH HER WE CAN KEEP HER AWAY FROM JINGLES-- ER, JIMMY!

HEY, SUMMER! LET'S GO TO THE MALL!
SOUNDS LIKE FUN!

Oh, THERE'S CHERYL BLOSSOM!
LET'S AVOID HER!
9

WHO'S SHE TALKING TO?
UH-OH! GUESS WHO?

LOOK AT HIM DROOLING OVER HER!
SHE HAS A BOYFRIEND! YOU DON'T HAVE TO WORRY!

NOT ANY-MORE!
ZAP

WHERE'D HE GO?!
I'M UP HERE!
POOF

HOW'D YOU DO THAT?
SOME-ONE PUT ME HERE!

I'M OUTTA HERE!
YOU WANNA PLAY? LET'S PLAY!!
10

ZOINK
ZAP

THOSE TWO ARE RECKLESSLY THROWING THEIR MAGIC AROUND!
WE HAVE TO MAKE SURE NOBODY SEES THIS!

I'VE PUT TOO MUCH RESPONSIBILITY ON THOSE GIRLS!
I'LL HAVE TO HANDLE THIS MYSELF!

C'MON, DEAR...
WE HAVE TO ROUND UP A COUPLE OF LOVESICK FOOLS!

SOON...
JIMMY! IT'S TIME TO COME HOME! LISTEN TO YOUR FATHER!
YOU'RE NOT MY--

YIPES! IT'S SANTA IN DISGUISE!
COMING, DADDY!

YOU NEED TO COME HOME WITH YOUR AUNTIE!
YES, MRS. CLAU-- ER, I MEAN AUNTIE!

HAVE A NICE DAY, LADIES! SORRY FOR ANY INCONVENIENCE!

WHO WERE THEY?
I THINK THEY WERE SANTA AND MRS. CLAUS!

I GUESS THEY HAD TO ROUND THOSE TWO UP WITHOUT DRAWING ATTENTION!
TOO LATE!

I WONDER IF HE'LL BANISH THEM FROM RIVERDALE?
GEE! WHAT IF WE NEVER SEE THEM AGAIN?

DON'T COUNT ON IT!
END

Sugar Plum thinks the girls are being manipulated by Archie; while Jingles thinks Archie would be better off without them. They each decide to take matters into their diminutive hands—by taking human forms to distract the teens!

FWAP
AND HERE'S THE TOP OF SANTA'S NAUGHTY LIST!
Oh, COME NOW!
NAUGHTY IS A SUBJECTIVE TERM!
I'M JUST A BIT... MISCHIEVOUS!
WALK ME HOME, ARCHIE!
DON'T BE RUDE, RON! HE'S ALREADY WALKING ME HOME!
CHOOSE, ARCHIEKINS!
WHO DO YOU WANT TO WALK HOME?
BOTH OF YOU, OF COURSE!
FORGET IT! YOU CAN'T HAVE IT BOTH WAYS!
2

SINCE WHEN?
SINCE NOW!
POOF
SUGAR PLUM!
I'M HERE TO SET YOU GIRLS STRAIGHT FOR THE NEW YEAR!
STOP LETTING THIS BOZO CONTROL YOU!
THERE ARE LOTS OF OTHER FISH IN THE SEA!
HEY!
WHY DON'T YOU MIND YOUR OWN BUSINESS?
POOF
JINGLES!
ARCHIE'S THE ONE BEING CONTROLLED BY THESE TWO PUPPET-MASTERS!
SO SAYS THE MALE CHAUVINIST ELF!
3

COME ON, YOU TWO!
WE CAN HANDLE OURSELVES!
DON'T YOU BOTH HAVE CHRISTMAS CHEER TO SPREAD ELSEWHERE?
WELL...
BYE, YOU TWO!
AND MERRY CHRISTMAS!
THAT POOR SAP! WHAT KIND OF A FUTURE WILL HE HAVE?
THOSE GIRLS CAN DO MUCH BETTER!
HMMM! I'VE GOT AN IDEA!
UH, SEE YOU LATER, GIRLIE!
BYE, JINGLES!
4

I'LL DISTRACT THOSE GIRLS FROM ARCHIE!
THAT'LL FREE HIM UP TO FIND SOMEONE BETTER!
I'LL POSE AS MY ALTER-EGO JIMMY, WITH A LITTLE ELF MAGIC!*
* JINGLES TRANSFORMED BEFORE IN "HOLIDAY WATCH"
JUST TRY AND RESIST MY ELFIN CHARM, BETTY AND VERONICA!
I'LL TRANSFORM MYSELF INTO A HUMAN-LOOKING TEEN! LET'S SEE IF I CAN DO THIS!
BOING
NOT BAD, GIRL! NOT BAD!
I'LL GO BY THE NAME SUMMER!
5

I'LL MAKE ARCHIE FLIP FOR ME!
THEN I'LL EXPOSE HIM FOR THE CAD HE IS!
MAYBE THAT'LL GET THOSE GIRLS TO WAKE UP AND SMELL THE COFFEE!
SO...
OH, LOOK! THERE HE IS!
AS HANDSOME AS EVER!
WELL, YOU KNOW... WHAT CAN I SAY...
JIMMY! YOU'RE BACK! WHERE HAVE YOU BEEN?!
HUH?!!
MY FAMILY MOVED OUT OF TOWN!
BUT I'M BACK NOW!
POP'S
6

GO TO THE CHRISTMAS BALL WITH ME!!
WOW!
I SAW HIM FIRST!
IN YOUR DREAMS!
GIRLS! YOU'RE FIGHTING OVER ME JUST LIKE BEFORE!*
* "HOLIDAY WATCH"
LET'S ALL GO! I'LL DANCE WITH BOTH OF YOU!
OKAY!
BOY! THOSE TWO ARE PRETTY FICKLE! MAYBE JINGLES WAS RIGHT!
IT'S WORKING ALREADY!
AT THE BALL...
LOOK AT THOSE GIRLS FALLING ALL OVER HIM!
HOW PATHETIC!
EXCUSE ME...

WOULD YOU LIKE TO DANCE?
WELL, ER... I'M NOT REALLY INTER...
BOING
LET'S GO!!

POP
EEEEEEKK!!
VERY FUNNY!
HAHA HA!
I THOUGHT SO!
WHAT'S ALL THE COMMOTION OVER HERE?
WE'RE JUST CHECKING OUT THIS GIRL WHO'S GETTING HER CLAWS INTO ARCHIE!
THE NAME'S SUMMER!
AND RED IS MY DATE FOR TONIGHT!
IS THIS TRUE?
WHAT DO YOU GIRLS CARE? YOU'RE BUSY WITH JIMMY!
NOW LISTEN HERE--!
NO, YOU LISTEN--!

AH! THEY'RE ALL FIGHTING AMONGST EACH OTHER!

MUSIC TO MY EARS!

WOW! SHE'S CUTE!

NOW THAT MY WORK IS DONE, MAYBE I CAN GET TO KNOW JIMMY!

WOULD YOU LIKE TO DANCE?

WHY, I'D LOVE TO!

YOU HAVE A CERTAIN... MAGICAL QUALITY!

I FEEL THE SAME ABOUT YOU!

AND TO THINK I THOUGHT YOU WERE SUCH A NICE GUY!
WAIT! NEVER MIND THEM!
LET'S FOCUS ON US!
WELLLL...
HMMM! YOU HAVE SOME POINTY EARS!
YEAH! JUST FOCUS ON MY CUTE FACE AND WE'LL BE FINE!
POINTY EARS... MAGICAL QUALITY...
ARE YOU JINGLES?!
WHAT?! HOW WOULD YOU KNOW THAT?!
OH! UH... JUST A WILD GUESS!
YOUR ANTENNAE ARE SHOWING... SUGAR PLUM!!
YANK

OF ALL THE RIDICULOUS THINGS!
I ONLY HAVE ONE THING TO SAY TO YOU...
SMOOCH
WELL! WILL YOU LOOK AT THOSE TWO!
HONESTLY!
SOME PEOPLE ARE JUST SO FICKLE!
END

When Jingles and the Sugar Plum Fairy reveal that Reggie has made the "naughty list," it's up to Archie and his friends to turn things around for Riverdale's resident prankster. Can they prove to Santa that Reggie's done a good deed before Christmas Eve?!

THAT'S ME!
READY FOR SOME HOLIDAY FUN?
WELL, YEAH...
DEPENDS ON THE FOOD!

JUST DON'T INVITE REGGIE!
WHY NOT?

HE'S ON THE LIST! NO PRESENTS FOR KIDS WHO BEHAVE BADLY!
NAUGHTY
REGINALD MANTLE
#13 --ON SANTA'S NAUGHTY LIST

THE GOOD NEWS IS, I DON'T HAVE TO MAKE ANOTHER VANITY MIRROR!
THIS IS TERRIBLE...
YET PREDICT-ABLE.

THERE'S GOT TO BE SOMETHING WE COULD DO TO HELP HIM, JINGLES!
WELL... THERE IS THE NAUGHTY CLAUSE...
?!
2

MEANWHILE...
THE NAUGHTY CLAUSE?!
Oh, DEAR!

SUGARPLUM THE FAIRY, SPILL IT!
I SHOULDN'T HAVE SAID A THING!
?!!

POOF

I HATE TO SAY THIS, BETTY, BUT...
WE NEED TO HELP REGGIE!

LATER, AT THE CHOCKLIT SHOPPE...

AT DILTON'S LAB...

IT'S JUST A SIDE PROJECT I'VE BEEN WORKING ON...

...A MOBILE ***GEODESIC DOME*** WITH SNOW CAMOUFLAGE!

YOU MADE THIS IN YOUR ***SPARE TIME,*** DILTON?

I HAD A TERRIBLE TIME FINDING PRESENTS FOR YOU GUYS THAT MATCH YOUR MIDDLE CLASS STYLE!

WHAT'S WITH THE GIANT ITALIAN ICE?

Oh, THAT? IT'S GONNA TAKE US TO THE NORTH POLE. WE'RE GONNA CONVINCE SANTA TO TRIM HIS NAUGHTY LIST!

SANTA, eh? YOU DIMWITS COULDN'T FINAGLE YOUR WAY INTO HIS GOOD GRACES?

LET'S ROLL! I DON'T WANT TO SPEND MY ENTIRE CHRISTMAS EVE SAVING YOUR HOLIDAY!
GOOD LUCK, GUYS!
6

NORTH POLE, HERE WE COME!!

A LITTLE WHILE INTO THEIR JOURNEY...
POOF
WHAT DO YOU KIDS THINK YOU'RE DOING?
WE'RE HOPING TO TALK TO SANTA ABOUT...WELL, YOU KNOW.
YEAH, TREASURE TROLL. I'M GONNA SAVE CHRISTMAS FOR ONE OF MY FRIENDS HERE.
Oh, DEAR. SANTA'S NOT GOING TO BE HAPPY!
Shush, SUGARPLUM!
WHAT'S SHE TALKING ABOUT?
SIGH!
WE'RE IN DEEP TROUBLE IF SANTA FINDS OUT THAT YOU'RE COMING TO VISIT!
WHO INVITED TWEEDLE-DUM AND LOSERPLUM? WE CAN HANDLE EL GORDO OURSELVES!
WELL, I NEVER--!
MY SENTIMENTS EXACTLY. WE'RE OUTTA HERE!
8

SOMETHING'S WRONG!
YOU MEAN ASIDE FROM THE FACT THAT WE'RE INSIDE OF A GIANT SNOWBALL?
AND WE'RE HITTING A BAD STORM!
SEATBELTS, EVERY-ONE! THIS SNOWBALL'S ABOUT TO SPLATTER!
AND I'M NOT WEARING WATER-PROOF MAS-CARA!
KA-POOFF
UGH!
EVERY-ONE OKAY?
I--I THINK SO...
I'M FINE, BETTY. ARE YOU?
POOF
?
9

NORTH POLE
WELCOME TO THE NORTH POLE, KIDS!
THANKS FOR THE SAVE, JINGLES!
DON'T THANK US YET! WE COULD GET INTO BIG TROUBLE. WE NEED TO SNEAK YOU IN!
HOW DO WE DO THAT? PRETEND WE'RE ELVES?
10

oh, NO!

CANDY FACTORY

SERIOUSLY, GUYS-- YOU'D EXPECT ME TO PASS **THIS** UP?

HE DOES HAVE A POINT!

CANDY FACTO

IT WAS WORTH IT!

JINGLES AND SUGARPLUM, YOU SNUCK THESE KIDS IN ON OUR BUSIEST DAY OF THE YEAR?! DO YOU HAVE ANYTHING TO SAY FOR YOURSELVES?!

I DIDN'T THINK SO! HAVE THE REINDEER TAKE THEM BACK TO RIVERDALE!

WHAT?!

THE REINDEER?! MISSING?!

GO FIND THEM!
IF WE DON'T, NO ONE WILL GET THEIR CHRISTMAS PRESENTS!
14

A LITTLE WHILE INTO THEIR SEARCH...

THE REINDEER! THEY'RE IMMOBILIZED BY THIS ICY SNOW! THINK, REGGIE!

MAYBE MY VANITY MIRROR AND A LITTLE SUN CAN DEFROST THE GIANT DOGS!

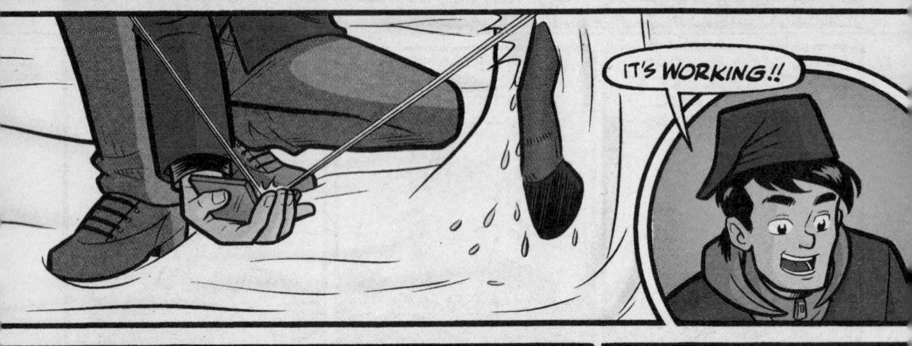
IT'S WORKING!!

A LITTLE WHILE AFTER...
AND VOILÀ! ALL DONE! WHAT DO WE SAY?

BLECHH! SO MUCH FOR FIXING MY HAIR!

Oh, THANK GOODNESS! THEY'RE ALRIGHT!

WOW, REGGIE, YOU SAVED CHRISTMAS!

REGGIE, I CAN'T BEGIN TO THANK YOU! AND BECAUSE OF THE *NAUGHTY CLAUSE*, YOU'LL...

YOU'LL, *uh*... MAKE ONE OF YOUR FRIENDS ***VERY*** HAPPY THIS YEAR.!

LEAST I CAN DO FOR THESE LOSERS, CLAUS.

THE NEXT DAY, A CHRISTMAS PARTY AMONG FRIENDS...
REGGIE, WHY ARE YOU LEAVING SO SOON?
HEY, I MET MY OBLIGATIONS, BETTS! YOUR PRESENTS ARE UNDER THE TREE... I GOT OTHER PARTIES TO HIT!
PLUS, YOU GUYS OWE ME BIG. I SAVED CHRISTMAS FOR ONE OF YOU! PROBABLY ALL OF YOU!

YOU SELFISH JERK! YOU WERE THE ONE ON THE NAUGHTY LIST! THEY SAVED YOUR CHRISTMAS!
I KNOW.
WOW! REGGIE SHOULDN'T HAVE!
HOW DID HE KNOW I WANTED THIS?
WHAT?! YOU KNEW?
I'M NOT GREAT AT SAYING THANK YOU. BUT I KNOW I HAVE THE BEST FRIENDS IN THE WORLD.
WELL, LOOKS LIKE THE NAUGHTY CLAUSE STILL WORKS!

HAPPY HOLIDAYS
FROM—
ARCHIE AND THE GANG!
R

Archie's FAVORITE Christmas Comics

ONCE UPON A YULETIDE

Imaginative tales filled with magical wonder and flights of fantasy have been a mainstay since the earliest days of Archie Comics. Archie and his friends have appeared in a host of "what if" stories as everything from clobbering cavemen to daydreaming youngsters, from olden fairy tale heroes to star-spanning, futuristic adventurers, and everything in-between! This pair of holiday tales carries on the tradition of imagining "what if?"... delivering some very special Christmas magic along the way!

A CHILDREN'S STORY
***The Adventures of Little Archie #29*, Winter 1963-64**
by Dexter Taylor

LET IT SNOW
***Archie's Weird Mysteries #18*, 2002**
by Paul Castiglia, Fernando Ruiz, Rich Koslowski, Stephanie Vozzo and Vickie Williams

This whimsical Little Archie tale imagines a planet almost completely populated by children. The only adult is Santa Claus! Just wait until you see how Santa and his elves get around!

...THEY ALL WRITE LETTERS TO THE **ONLY ADULT** ON THE PLANET....

MAIL
NORTH POLE
YIII! LOOK AT ALL THESE LETTERS!

EACH CHRISTMAS EVE ALL THE INHABITANTS DISPLAY THEIR STOCKINGS AND GO TO BED...
FOR SANTA

FOR THIS OCCASION SANTA REQUIRES MANY HELPERS....
REVIEWING

...HAVING NO REINDEER ON THIS PLANET, SANTA'S HELPERS RIDE IN **ROCKET SLEDS** POWERED FROM FUEL MADE FROM CHEMISTRY SETS....
CHEMISTRY SET

CHRISTMAS EVE, MEN! TO YOUR SLEDS!
2.

THIS PARTICULAR FUEL WAS PUT IN **SANTA'S OWN SLED...**

THE MIGHTY ENGINE THRUST SENDS SANTA'S SLED SOARING PAST MILLIONS OF STARS...

...AND INTO THE GRAVITATIONAL PULL OF EARTH...

WHEW! GETTING SORTA WARM!

WHAT ODDLY SHAPED STRUCTURES!

GUESS I'LL FIND OUT WHERE I AM!

BUMP!

HMM... A STRANGE DOORWAY!
4

GRRR

STOP, SPOTTY, THAT'S SANTA CLAUS!
A CHILD! I MUST BE BACK ON PLANET PEEWEE AGAIN!
SNAP!

WHO'S YOUR FIERCE FRIEND BESIDE YOU?
SPOTTY? HE'S MY BEST FRIEND! HE'S A DOG!

DOG?. THEY DON'T HAVE DOGS ON PLANET PEEWEE! WHERE COULD I HAVE LANDED?
RIVERDALE, U.S.A., PLANET EARTH! MY NAME IS LITTLE ARCHIE!

TONIGHT ISN'T CHRISTMAS EVE, EITHER?
GOLLY, NO, SANTA, BUT IT WILL BE SOON!
5

B-BUT **HOW** DID YOU KNOW WHO I WAS?
WE HAVE A SANTA CLAUS ON THIS PLANET, TOO!

IS THAT SO? WELL, WHAT DO YOU WANT FOR CHRISTMAS? PERHAPS I COULD PUT IN A GOOD WORD!

NOTHING! THE BEST PART OF CHRISTMAS IS GIVING PRESENTS TO SOMEONE ELSE!
EH! **SOMETHING FOR SOMEONE ELSE!** THIS **IS** A **DIFFERENT WORLD!**

IN MY WORLD THE CHILDREN GIVE ME A LIST A COUPLE OF MILES LONG! I WANT THIS! I WANT THAT! AFTER CHRISTMAS I'M A NERVOUS WRECK!

DO YOU THINK YOU COULD PLANT THE IDEA OF **GIVING** IN THEIR MINDS?
HMMM.... I SUPPOSE I COULD....

NOW LET **ME** HELP **YOU!** MAYBE I COULD SUPPLY A PRESENT FOR SOMEONE FROM YOU!
6

I COULD USE AN ELECTRIC SHAVER FOR ONE OF THE FAMILY!
HERE'S ONE THAT CUTS THE OL' WHISKERS!

GOSH! HE'LL REALLY GO FOR THIS! THANKS!
GLAD I COULD HELP! NOW I SEE IT'S TIME FOR ME TO GO!

MERRY CHRISTMAS, LITTLE ARCHIE!
MERRY CHRISTMAS, SANTA!

WHAT A GOOD BOY! THAT'S A PRESENT HIS DEAR OL' DAD WILL REALLY LIKE!

AND BACK ON EARTH....

TO SPOTTY WHOSE WHISKERS ALWAYS GET IN HIS MILK! Little Archie
END

From the pages of* Archie's Weird Mysteries *comes a mystery of a different sort, as Jack Frost and his friends from the Weatherworld set out to grant a little girl's wish for a white Christmas!

SCRIPT: PAUL CASTIGLIA PENCILS: FERNANDO RUIZ INKING: RICH KOSLOWSKI LETTERING: VICKIE WILLIAMS COLORING: STEPHANIE VOZZO

...THERE WAS A WONDERFUL KINGDOM CALLED WEATHERWORLD...
OLD MAN WINTER
WIND JILL
JACK FROST
SPRING THAW
...FILLED WITH MAGICAL CREATURES WHO CONTROLLED EARTH'S WEATHER!
BUT THINGS ON WEATHERWORLD WEREN'T ALWAYS MAGICAL AND WONDERFUL...
I THOUGHT I'D FIND YOU HERE... HEY, WHY SO DOWN, JACK?
JUST LOOK AT THOSE MONITORS--WHAT DO... OR DON'T... YOU SEE?
I SEE QUAINT LITTLE TOWNS DECORATED FOR THE HOLIDAYS!
YES, BUT LACKING THE MOST BEAUTIFUL HOLIDAY DECORATION OF ALL...
DOESN'T EVERYONE DESERVE A WHITE CHRISTMAS?
2

NOW, JACK, YOU KNOW THERE'S NOTHING WE CAN DO ABOUT WARM-WEATHER CLIMATES. BESIDES, THE FOLKS WHO LIVE THERE EXPECT SNOWLESS WINTERS...
I SUPPOSE... BUT I'M SURE THEY DON'T ALL LIKE THEM...
...AND JACK WAS RIGHT. NO ONE LIKED IT LESS THAN LITTLE ASHLEY COLLINS...
OH, HOW I WISH IT WOULD SNOW-- JUST ONCE, LIKE ON ALL THE CHRISTMAS SPECIALS!
AND EVERY CHANCE SHE GOT...
GO AHEAD, DEAR-- BLOW OUT THE CANDLES AND MAKE A WISH!
I WISH IT WOULD SNOW ON CHRISTMAS!
...SHE HOPED AND WISHED FOR A WHITE CHRISTMAS!
THAT'S IT, ASHLEY--TOSS THEM INTO THE WISHING WELL!
PLEASE LET IT SNOW THIS CHRISTMAS!
ASHLEY, HOW COULD SUCH A HEARTWARMING HOLIDAY SPECIAL MAKE YOU CRY?!
IT'S NOT FAIR-- EVERYONE ELSE GETS TO PLAY WITH SNOW AT CHRISTMAS-TIME!
THIS HAPPENS EVERY YEAR--I DON'T KNOW WHY WE LET HER WATCH THESE SPECIALS IN THE FIRST PLACE!
OH, THAT'S HEARTBREAKING!
ISN'T IT TERRIBLE? THERE MUST BE SOME WAY WE CAN BRIGHTEN THAT LITTLE GIRL'S HOLIDAYS...
3

JILL, REMEMBER HOW YOU HELPED ME FREEZE OVER RIVERDALE...?
...UM... YES...
WELL, I NEED YOU TO HELP ME AGAIN!
BUT, JACK, THAT WAS HORRIBLE--YOU PARALYZED A WHOLE TOWN!
I'M NOT TALKING ABOUT ANOTHER ICE AGE...
I DON'T KNOW...
SHE'D LIKE THAT!
NO... SHE'D LOVE IT!
I JUST WANT TO GIVE THAT GIRL A LITTLE TASTE OF WINTER...
OH, THAT POOR, SWEET GIRL...
SHE WOULD LOVE IT, BUT IT'S NOT GOING TO HAPPEN!
4

BUT, SIR--THAT SWEET LITTLE GIRL IS HEART-BROKEN!
I KNOW, AND I FEEL SORRY FOR HER, BUT... YOU KNOW WE'RE NOT ALLOWED TO USE OUR POWERS TO ALTER THE NATURAL ORDER OF THINGS!
THOSE CLIMATES ARE SUPPOSED TO STAY WARM AND SNOWLESS, UNLESS MOTHER NATURE SAYS OTHERWISE, UNDERSTAND?
YES, SIR.
OH, NO--WHAT DID THEY DO, ARCHIE?
YEAH, JUST LIKE WE TELL OUR MOMMY WHEN WE HAVE PROBLEMS!
COULDN'T THEY JUST TELL MOTHER NATURE THEIR PROBLEM?
THEY THOUGHT OF THAT, BUT MOTHER NATURE HAD THE DAY OFF AND DIDN'T WANT TO BE DISTURBED!
THEY NEVER GAVE UP HOPE, HOWEVER, AND SOON...
JILL, COME HERE, QUICK--I THINK I FOUND A SOLUTION!
AFTER ALL, THE OLD MAN ONLY SAID WE COULDN'T USE OUR OWN POWERS TO MAKE A WHITE CHRISTMAS...
SUNNEY VALL
SKI LODGE
"SKI ALL YEAR
LONG! ARTIFICI
SNOW MADE
DAILY!"
JUST WHAT DOES JACK HAVE IN MIND? KEEP READING FOR THE "CHILLING" CONCLUSION!
5

DETERMINED TO GIVE ASHLEY A HAPPY, SNOW-FILLED HOLIDAY, JACK FLIES TO EARTH WITH WIND JILL AND SPRING THAW...
LET IT SNOW!
CHAPTER TWO
THAT'S ASHLEY'S HOUSE DOWN THERE!
OH, JACK-- I HOPE THIS WORKS!
I'M STILL NOT SURE WHY YOU ASKED ME--ESPECIALLY AT 4 IN THE MORNING....
YOU'LL KNOW SOON ENOUGH, SPRING...
ENOUGH CHAT, GALS--WE'VE GOT TO GET TO THE SKI LODGE!
6

SOON...
...THERE'S THE SKI LODGE...
...AND THERE'S THE SNOW MACHINE. FEELING STRONG TODAY, SPRING?
WHAT?! YOU BROUGHT ME HERE FOR ADDED MUSCLE?!

WELL, THAT'S NOT THE ONLY REASON...
NOT TO MENTION, DID YOU GET PERMISSION TO BORROW THIS?
WE'LL HAVE IT BACK BEFORE SUNRISE!
7

AFTER TOUCHING DOWN IN ASHLEY'S YARD...
OKAY, GIRLS--GET THAT SNOW MACHINE STARTED--I'LL GO GET ASHLEY...
WELL, THIS IS A CHANGE OF PACE FOR YOU, SPRING!
YES, INDEED--I'M USUALLY MELTING, NOT MAKING, SNOW!
DON'T BE AFRAID, SWEETHEART. I'M JACK FROST, AND I'VE BROUGHT SNOW FOR YOU TO PLAY WITH!
SNOW... HERE?
HOLD ON TIGHT, ASHLEY!
WHEEEEEEEEE!!!
LET'S CATCH SNOWFLAKES ON OUR TONGUES!
I'VE ALWAYS WANTED TO BUILD A SNOWMAN!
Hmmm... THAT FACE LOOKS... FAMILIAR!
8

GO AHEAD, ASHLEY --YOU CAN DO IT!
HEE HEE!
HEY, NICE SHOT, ASHLEY!
DON'T YOU MEAN "ICE SHOT"?!
YOU ARE, WITHOUT A DOUBT, THE MOST ADORABLE ANGEL!
SHE'S NOT THE ONLY ANGEL HERE, RIGHT, JACK?!
I HAVE TO TAKE ASHLEY BACK IN NOW. JILL, YOU CAN TELL SPRING WHY WE BROUGHT HER NOW...
OKAY. SPRING, WE NEED YOU TO THAW THIS ALL BEFORE SUNRISE. NO HUMANS CAN FIND OUT WE DID THIS!
GOTCHA! IT WILL BE MY PLEASURE!
AND SO, AFTER JACK SAFELY RETURNS ASHLEY TO BED AND SPRING THAWS THE YARD...
BUT WILL THAT BE ENOUGH FOR HER?
YOU SAW THE LOOK ON HER FACE --IT WAS MAGICAL! I'D SAY WE SUCCEEDED!
I TOLD HER IT WAS ALL A DREAM... YOU KNOW THE POWER OF SUGGESTION!
9

AND SO, CHRISTMAS MORNING ARRIVES, AND AFTER THE GIFTS ARE OPENED...
I BETTER THROW OUT THIS WRAPPING PAPER NOW BEFORE I FORGET ...HUH?! ICICLES?! HERE IN SUNNY VALLEY? WHAT A WEIRD MYSTERY!

BUT IT WASN'T A MYSTERY TO ASHLEY, WHO HAD THE MERRIEST CHRISTMAS EVER!
HOW DO YOU LIKE YOUR PRESENTS, HONEY?
I LOVE THEM, BUT I ALREADY GOT THE BEST GIFT OF ALL--I DREAMED IT SNOWED!

THE END!
YAY! ASHLEY GOT TO PLAY WITH SNOW, AFTER ALL!
THANK YOU FOR THE STORY, ARCHIE!
THAT WAS THE BEST CHRISTMAS STORY EVER!
ARCHIE, KIDS--COME HERE, QUICK!

THAT WASN'T THERE BEFORE!
GUESS YOU'D CALL THAT "FREEZE-MAIL"!
SEASONS GREETINGS EVERYON

WHO SAYS WORKING ON THE HOLIDAYS ISN'T FUN?
HAPPY HOLIDAYS, WEIRD-BELIEVERS!

SABRINA
in
"HANGING HANG-UP"

AUNT HILDA, I CAN'T PLACE THE STAR ON TOP OF THE TREE.!

SABRINA, WHAT DO YOU THINK YOU'RE A WITCH FOR?

END.

SABRINA
in
FOTO FUN

SIGH! SABRINA, THIS PHOTO BRINGS BACK MEMORIES!
SABRINA'S PHOTO ALBUM

WHICH ONE?

YOUR FIRST SNOWWITCH!
END.

Archie's FAVORITE Christmas Comics

WINTER WONDERLAND

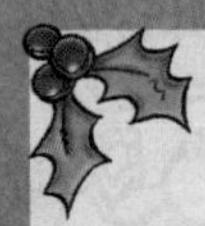

It seems every year brings a "White Christmas" to Riverdale... and there's no fun like "snow fun" when Archie and his pals are involved! The wintry weather has provided many the backdrop for frosty, frantic fun! This trio of tales presents both conventional (skis, a snowmobile) and unconventional (horse-drawn sleigh, shopping cart) ways that the intrepid teens choose to traverse the snowy terrain!

SKI-CART CATASTROPHE
***Laugh Comics #300*, 1976**
by George Gladir, Sal Amendola, Jon D'Agostino, Barry Grossman and Bill Yoshida

SLAY RIDE
***Archie Giant Series #5*, 1958**
by Frank Doyle and Harry Lucey

FROSTY FAIRY TALES
***Betty & Veronica #120*, 1998**
by Mike Pellowski, Dan DeCarlo, Barry Grossman and Bill Yoshida

Archie and Jughead are convinced their rigged-up shopping cart is the only way to get around in the snow... but when it picks up speed it's less of a shopping cart and more of a kart racer!

Jughead in SKI-CART CATASTROPHE

Script: George Gladir / Pencils: Sal Amendola / Inks: Jon D'Agostino / Letters: Bill Yoshida / Colors: Barry Grossman

VERY IMPRESSIVE!
BETTY, IT'S THE LATEST FAD IN WINTER SPORTS!
ARCHIE, TELL ME--- DOES IT WORK?
DON'T KNOW! JUGHEAD IS GOING TO TEST IT NOW!
JUGGIE, WHY DID YOU VOLUNTEER TO TEST THIS MONSTROSITY?
ARCHIE OFFERED ME TEN BURGERS!
BUT WHAT IF THE SKI-CART HAS AN ACCIDENT?
NO PROBLEM, BETTY!
I ALREADY ATE THE BURGERS!
JUG, YOU'RE CRAZY TO RIDE THIS CART FOR TEN BURGERS!
I SHOULD HAVE HELD OUT FOR TWELVE?
2

OHHHHH--- WHAT'S THE USE?
READY?
READY!

BE VERY CAREFUL, JUGHEAD!
I DON'T WANT YOU TO DAMAGE THE SKI-CART!
WHOOSH!!

IT'S WORKING! IT'S WORKING!
GASP! I DON'T BELIEVE IT!
HMMMM--- NOT BAD! THIS SKI-CART IS A LOT OF FUN!

WHIIZZZ!
HA! HA! BETTY THOUGHT THE SKI-CART WAS DANGEROUS! YUK! YUK!

TWANG!!
WHOMP!
3

I KNEW HE'D HAVE AN ACCIDENT!
IT DOESN'T LOOK SERIOUS!
I HOPE NOTHING'S BROKEN!

WE'RE IN LUCK!
WE ARE ???

YEAH! THE SKI-CART'S ALL RIGHT! NOTHING'S BROKEN!
PAT! PAT!

ER---ARCH, I DON'T THINK THE SKI-CART'S SAFE!
LISTEN TO THE MAN, ARCHIE!

NONSENSE! JUG'S MERELY A CLUMSY DRIVER!
WATCH HOW IT HANDLES UNDER MY EXPERIENCED HANDS!
4

SAY-Y--- THIS *IS* FUN! IT'S A *GREAT* RIDE!

ULP!
?

YIPES!!! THE LAKE!!!

SPLATTERY!!!

EVERYTHING COMES *FROZEN* TODAY!
YOU'RE NOT KIDDING!
R-MARKET
FROZEN FO
PIZZA
MIXED FRUITS
PEAS & CARROTS
END.

A blizzardy night is not about to stop Archie from attending the Lodge Christmas party... especially since he's playing Santa Claus! Archie travels via a one horse sleigh... and if you think the real Santa knows how to make an entrance wait until you see Archie's!

I HIRED THIS RIG AT SAM'S RIDING ACADEMY!
ONLY JUGHEAD WOULD GET AN IDEA LIKE THIS!
TERRIFIC!

TO MISS VERONICA'S MY GOOD MAN!
JINGLE BELLS JINGLE BELLS
MUSH!

CHRISTMAS EVE! IT ALWAYS MAKES ME ALL TINGLY!
-ESPECIALLY A WHITE CHRISTMAS!

TALLY-HO, LADIES!
YULE TIDE GREETINGS!
MERRY CHRISTMAS, FELLOWS!

DID YOU GET YOUR CAR THROUGH THAT SNOW?
HA! -TELL HIM, JUGHEAD!

A FRIEND OF MINE BROUGHT US OVER, SIR! COME OUTSIDE AND MEET HIM!

IN THIS COLD? -NEVER!
BRING HIM IN!

ER- NO, MR. LODGE! - I DON'T THINK---
PLEASE, ARCH! YOU HEARD OUR HOST!

JUG! -Y-YOU WOULDN'T--?
QUIET, ARCHIE!

BRING YOUR FRIEND IN IMMEDIATELY, SON!
YES, SIR!

WHERE ARE YOUR MANNERS, ARCHIE? HOW COULD YOU EVEN THINK OF LEAVING SOMEONE---
CLOMP!
CLOMP!

--OUTSIDE--IN THIS--WEATHER!
DOBBIN-MEET MR. LODGE!

HERE I COME! -READY OR NOT!

WOOSH!

IDIOT!
WELL, HE INSISTED!

HOP IN!
NO, THANKS! -WE'LL WALK!

C'MON, DOBBIN! -I'LL GET YOU BACK BEFORE I GET CHARGED FOR ANOTHER HOUR!

BOY!-WHAT SNOW! IT'S GOING TO BE SOME JOB GETTING BACK TO RONNIE'S TONIGHT TO DELIVER OUR GIFTS!
YEAH, AND ME IN A SANTA CLAUS SUIT!

PLOUGHING THROUGH THIS MESS IN THAT SUIT WILL BE---
HEY! -WAIT!

ARE YOU THINKING WHAT I'M THINKING?
SURE! WE CAN RENT THE RIG THAT JUG HAD!

I'LL STOP AT SAM'S RIDING ACADEMY NOW! I'LL SEE YOU TONIGHT!
BE AT MY PLACE EARLY! I THINK I KNOW HOW WE CAN IMPROVE ON THIS IDEA!

PUTTING ON A LITTLE WEIGHT, SON?
HA! HA! MINE IS FAKED POP!

HO, HO, HO! MERRR-RY CHRISTMAS EVERYBODY!

REGGIE MANTLE! HAVE YOU BEEN A GOOD BOY THIS YEAR?
YOK! YOK! -AS GOOD AS YOU!

LOOK AT THIS, ARCH! THE CROWNING TOUCH! -A REINDEER FOR SANTA!
TERRIFIC!

DOBBIN- YOUR NAME IS NOW "RUDOLPH"!

HEY! WHAT'S UP? STEALING MY STUFF?
LET'S HAVE THOSE GIFTS, JUG!

WE MIGHT AS WELL LET SANTA DELIVER OUR PRESENTS!
CAN WE TRUST HIM?

NOW YOU AND "RUDOLPH" TAKE A RIDE TO GIVE US TIME TO GET TO RONNIE'S!

SHOW UP IN ABOUT A HALF HOUR!
OKAY!

HO, HO, HO! -M-ERRRY CHRISTMAS! -M-E-RRY CHRISTMAS!

HA! HA! HI, SANTA!
WHAT YOU GOT FOR ME?

WHOA, DOBBIN! YOU SEEM TO BE STRAINING! I THINK SOMEBODY GOOFED UP THIS HARNESS!

HMM? LET'S SEE NOW! THIS IS A BIT LOOSE AND THIS STRAP HERE SEEMS TO NEED---
OH, OH!

WHOOPS! -D-DOBBIN! H-HOLD IT!
WHOA!

STOP!
DESIST!
HALT!
KNOCK IT OFF!

HALP!
YAHOO! -RIDE 'IM SANTA!
IS THAT SANTA CLAUS OR ANITA?

DOBBIN! R-RUDOLPH! HORSEY! HALP!
SAM'S RIDING

SCREE-EECH!

WAL, I'LL BE DING DANGED! IMAGINE YOU REMEMBERIN' AN OLD CODGER LIKE ME!
CHOMP CHOMP

NEVER MIND THE FUNNIES! HELP ME GET THIS NAG BACK TO THE SLEIGH!

HMPH! -DIDN'T LEAVE ME A THING! -I THINK I'LL STOP BELIEVIN' IN YOU!

AN' DON'T **YOU** EXPECT SPECIAL TREATMENT, DOBBIN, JUS' 'CAUSE YER SPORTIN' A NEW BONNET!
BOY, I'LL BET YOU'RE A RIOT AROUND THE STABLES!

WELL, THANKS, MISTER! -AND MERRY CHRISTMAS!
STINGY!

MEANWHILE....
IT'S GETTING LATE! WHAT HAPPENED TO ARCHIE?
HAH! OL' CARROT TOP'S GOT A SURPRISE FOR YOU!

HE'S NOT **COMING?**
YOU KNOW ARCH! HE LIKES TO MAKE AN **ENTRANCE!**

PERSONALLY, I PREFER HIS **EXITS!**

MAYBE HE'S COMING AS SANTA CLAUS AND GOT STUCK IN THE **CHIMNEY!**
HMM!

I THINK I'LL LIGHT A FIRE!

WE'RE ALMOST THERE DOBBIN! IT'S JUST OVER THIS HILL!

H-HEY!! S-SLOW DOWN!

YIPES! DOBBIN! HOLD IT! PUT ON THE BRAKES!

WHOA-A-A!

SCREECH!

WAP!

DADDY, DO YOU SUPPOSE ANYTHING HAPPENED TO KEEP ARCHIE FROM GETTING HERE?
EVEN AT CHRISTMAS I COULDN'T BE THAT LUCKY!
I THINK I CAN HEAR SLEIGHBELLS!

AIEEEEEE!

IT IS SLEIGHBELLS! HE'S COMIN'!
SOUNDS LIKE HE'S COMING AWFULLY FAST!
I TOLD YOU HE'D MAKE IT! WAIT'LL YOU SEE THIS ENTRANCE!

CRASH!

M-MERRY CHRISTMAS TO ALL!
EEP! - AND TO ALL, A GOOD NIGHT!
CHOMP! CHOMP!
The End

A trip to the slopes finds Betty and Veronica meeting boys in unusual circumstances—Betty fixes a cute guy's snowmobile, while Veronica can't shake a couple of pesky seventh grade skiers!

Betty and Veronica in "FROSTY FAIRY TALE"

BUT BETTY, ALL THE CUTE GUYS ARE ON THE SLOPES!

I STILL WANT TO GO SNOWMOBILING, RON!

Doyle / DeCarlo / Lapick / Yoshida / Grossman

I'LL MEET YOU BACK AT THE LODGE!
OKAY!

I'LL BE THE ONE WITH ALL THE HANDSOME GUYS AROUND ME!
RIGHT! THAT SOUNDS LIKE THE PERFECT FAIRY TALE ENDING TO YOUR DAY!
LIFT LINE

LATER ON THE SKI SLOPE...
NOW TO START CHECKING OUT ALL THE HANDSOME GUYS!
HEY, GORGEOUS!!

HUH?
WE JUST VOTED YOU THE MOST BEAUTIFUL SNOW BUNNY ON THE SLOPES!

WHAT IS THIS, A SIXTH GRADE SNOW CONVENTION?
NO WAY! WE'RE ON A 7TH GRADE SKI CLUB TRIP!
2

HEY! CHECK HER OUT! SHE'S PRETTY!
FORGET HER! CAN'T YOU SEE SHE'S BABY-SITTING HER LITTLE BROTHER?

WILL YOU BOYS PLEASE GO AWAY?
NOT UNTIL YOU TELL US YOUR NAME!

OKAY, OKAY! MY NAME IS VERONICA LODGE!
HEY, FELLAS! COME OVER AND MEET VERONICA LODGE!
YEAH!

MEANWHILE...
STAY ON THE *MARKED TRAILS*!
DON'T WORRY... I WILL!
RENTALS
SNO
3

I JUST LOVE SNOWMOBILING!

WHO CARES IF I DON'T MEET ANY BOYS... THIS IS FUN!

UH-OH! SOMEONE IS IN TROUBLE!
THIS DARN THING WON'T START!

HI! CAN I BE OF ANY HELP?
YOU WOULDN'T HAPPEN TO BE A MECHANIC, WOULD YOU? THE ENGINE STALLED AND LEFT ME STRANDED!

AS A MATTER OF FACT I WORK PART TIME AT A GARAGE! I KNOW A LOT ABOUT ENGINES!
WOW! BEAUTIFUL AND BRAINY!
4

LATER...
IT WAS JUST FLOODED! IT SHOULD START NOW! TRY IT!
YOU'RE A LIFE SAVER, BETTY! I OWE YOU BIG-TIME!
CLICK!
VAROOM!

YOU HAVE TO LET ME BUY YOU DINNER BACK AT THE LODGE! I WON'T TAKE NO FOR AN ANSWER!
THE THOUGHT OF REFUSING NEVER CROSSED MY MIND!

COME ON! I'LL RACE YOU BACK!
OKAY! YOU'RE ON!

BACK AT THE LODGE...
I WONDER WHERE RON IS? I HAVEN'T SEEN HER SINCE WE SPLIT UP!

OH! THERE SHE IS NOW... AND JUST LIKE SHE SAID, SHE'S SURROUNDED BY GUYS!
5

LET'S CUDDLE UP BY THE FIRE, RON!
CAN I BUY YOU A SODA?
BETTY! THANK GOODNESS! HELP ME GET RID OF THESE LITTLE PESTS!

SORRY, RON... NO CAN DO! I HAVE A DINNER DATE!
YOU DO? WITH WHO?

OH, A GUY I MET!
THERE'S MATT NOW! SEE YOU!
HUH? BETTY ENDS UP WITH PRINCE CHARMING!

AND I GET STUCK WITH THE SEVEN DWARFS! HMPH! SOME FROSTY FAIRY TALE THIS TURNED OUT TO BE!
HEY! YOU'RE NOT EXACTLY SNOW WHITE, EITHER!
END

Archie
SNOW-MOBILE SNUGGLE

Archie's FAVORITE Christmas Comics
Dan Parent
HOLIDAY PARTY TIME

Archie and his friends have always been up for a party—and Christmas time gives them even more reasons to celebrate! The fun and festive parties depicted in Archie Comics are so special because the friends often use their celebrations to open their hearts and give to each other as well as the less fortunate. This group of stories features the gang throwing parties that help the needy, orphans, each other and even each other's pets, all while having fun! And really, isn't that what Christmas is all about?

PARTY TIME
***Betty & Veronica Double Digest #176*, 2010**
by George Gladir, Jeff Shultz
and Jon D'Agostino

PARTY DOGS
***Betty & Veronica #222,* 2007**
by George Gladir, Jeff Shultz
and Al Milgrom

GIVE AND TAKE
***Archie Digest #258,* 2009**
by Dan Parent, Jim Amash
and Barry Grossman

THE PARTY
***Betty & Veronica Digest #189,* 2009**
by George Gladir, Jeff Shultz,
Jon D'Agostino, Jack Morelli
and Barry Grossman

Veronica is excited to throw one of her patently elaborate Christmas Eve parties, until Betty informs her all her guests are already committed to helping feed the needy that night. Will the Christmas spirit inspire a change of plans for Veronica?

Betty and Veronica in PARTY time!

MOTHER, WHAT DO YOU THINK OF THIS OUTFIT I HAD DESIGNED FOR THE CHRISTMAS EVE COSTUME PARTY I'M GIVING?

OH, IT'S ABSOLUTELY *SMASHING!*

Script: GEORGE GLADIR Pencils: JEFF SHULTZ Inks: JON D'AGOSTINO

BETTY COOPER TO SEE YOU, MISS VERONICA!
BETTY? I'LL BE RIGHT THERE!

RONNIE, I'VE BEEN TRYING TO CONTACT YOU FOR DAYS! YOU DON'T ANSWER YOUR E-MAIL OR CELL PHONE!

THAT'S BECAUSE I'VE BEEN BUSY PLANNING MY CHRISTMAS EVE COSTUME PARTY!
CHRISTMAS EVE COSTUME PARTY?!

BUT THE GANG HAS ALREADY VOLUNTEERED TO HELP FEED THE NEEDY ON CHRISTMAS EVE!
WHAT?!

GIRL, YOU JUST CAN'T DO THIS TO ME... I'VE BEEN PLANNING THIS PARTY FOR MONTHS!

YOU AND OUR FRIENDS WILL JUST HAVE TO RESCHEDULE FEEDING THE NEEDY!
I'M AFRAID IT'S MUCH TOO LATE FOR THAT!
2

VERONICA, I COULDN'T HELP BUT OVERHEAR YOUR CONVERSATION... NORMALLY I DON'T LIKE TO INTERFERE WITH YOUR PLANS...

...BUT I THINK YOU'RE BEING VERY UNREASONABLE IN TRYING TO GET YOUR WAY!

THESE ARE VERY DIFFICULT TIMES... CHRISTMAS EVE IS WHEN WE SHOULD BE THINKING OF OTHERS!

YOU'RE RIGHT, DADDY! IT'S THE NIGHT I SHOULD BE THINKING OF OTHERS...

...INSTEAD OF TRYING TO GET MY WAY! BUT I DID HAVE MY HEART SET ON WEARING THIS COSTUME TO MY PARTY!

I'LL CANCEL MY PARTY AND HELP WITH FEEDING THE NEEDY!
OH, RONNIE, I KNEW YOU'D SEE THE LIGHT!
3

CHRISTMAS EVE...
GANG, GET READY TO FEED THE NEEDY!
BUT WHERE'S VERONICA? SHE SAID SHE'D BE HERE AT SIX!

HERE I AM, GUYS!
YOU'RE WEARING YOUR COSTUME!

I THOUGHT IT WOULD LEND A FESTIVE NOTE TO THE OCCASION!
YOU'RE ABSOLUTELY CORRECT! IT IS CHRISTMAS EVE!

AND I ALSO BROUGHT SANTA HATS FOR ALL OF YOU TO WEAR!
THAT'S SO COOL, RONNIE!

YEAH! MY HAT'S OFF TO YOU AND YOUR SANTA HAT IDEA!
4

EVERYBODY SEEMS TO BE HAVING A FAB TIME!

EVERYBODY WILL BE EVEN HAPPIER WHEN DADDY ANNOUNCES HIS PLAN!
WHAT PLAN IS THAT?

LADIES AND GENTLEMEN, I KNOW THESE ARE DIFFICULT TIMES... I HOPE WHAT I'M ABOUT TO SAY WILL BRING SOME CHEER TO YOU!

I'M OPENING A NEW PLANT IN TOWN THAT I'M HOPING WILL CREATE JOBS FOR MANY OF YOU!

AND I MIGHT ADD, ESPECIALLY TO ALL YOU KIDS OUT THERE... LET'S PARTY AND CELEBRATE MY FATHER'S GOOD NEWS!

I EVEN BROUGHT THESE SPECIAL ELF COSTUMES FOR YOU KIDS TO WEAR TONIGHT!
5

LATER...
OKAY GANG, THIS IS THE WONDERFUL CAKE MY CHEF HAS BAKED ESPECIALLY FOR ALL YOU ELVES! NOW LET'S PARTY!
MERRY CHRISTMAS

SIR, LOOKS LIKE OUR FEEDING THE NEEDY HAS TURNED INTO A CHRISTMAS EVE COSTUME PARTY AFTER ALL!

YES, AND IT'S SO TYPICAL OF VERONICA...

...EVEN WHEN SHE DOESN'T GET HER WAY, SHE STILL MANAGES TO GET HER WAY!
6
THE END

It's a canine Christmas when Veronica throws a party for all of her friends' pooches! While the girls all have fun, it's "ruff" sledding for the doggies, who are up to their snouts in incessant pampering and tacky gifts!

I'M SO GLAD YOU ALL COULD COME WITH YOUR PETS TO MY YULE PARTY FOR DOGS!
BETTY DOESN'T HAVE A DOG, SO SHE'LL BE HELPING ME DISPENSE THE PARTY FAVORS!
WHERE'S THE PARTY CHOW!?

SCRIPT: GEORGE GLADIR
PENCILS: JEFF SHULTZ
INKS: AL MILGROM

Betty and Veronica in Party Dogs

WHY ARE YOU DUDES GIVING ME THAT STRANGE LOOK?!

YIPES! NOW I KNOW WHY!!

SORRY, TOMOKO! THAT IS THE SMALLEST HAT WE HAVE!
NEXT YEAR I'LL JUST HAVE TO BRING A BIG GREAT DANE!

AS YOU ALL KNOW, SOMETIMES DOGGIES SMELL TOO DOGGY...
...ESPECIALLY AFTER A RAIN!
I THINK THAT'S WHEN WE SMELL OUR BEST!

THIS SPECIAL COLOGNE DE CHIEN TAKES CARE OF THAT!
SPRITZ

Phew! AND CREATES A BRAND NEW PROBLEM!
...AND JUST WHEN I WAS MAKING HEADWAY WITH THAT CUTE LI'L CHIHUAHUA!!
2

THEY'LL LOVE IT ONCE THEY GET ACCUSTOMED TO THE SOPHISTICATED BOUQUET!
PSSSTTT
YIP
YIP
YIPE
KOFF KOFF

AND NOW FOR THE TREAT YOU'VE BEEN WAITING FOR!
THE FOOD!

THE PARISIAN-DESIGNED DOGGIE OUTFITS!
QUICK! WHERE'S THE NEAREST EXIT!?!

OH, HOT DOG! YOU'RE GOING TO LOOK SO CUNNING!
WHY ME? WHY ME?

NOW, IF YOU COULD ONLY SEE YOURSELF!
GULP! I DARE NOT LOOK IN THAT MIRROR AGAIN!!
3

DON'T WORRY, GUYS! YOUR TURN WILL COME!
NOW TO ATTIRE THE REST OF YOU!

HA! YOU DINGALINGS ARE NO LONGER LAUGHING!
AT LEAST VERONICA IS EVEN-HANDED!
HER OWN DOGS GET THE FULL TREATMENT!!

AND NOW FOR A GROUP PICTURE OF ALL OF YOU! SMILE!
I WONDER WHAT ROGUE'S GALLERY THE PHOTO IS GOING TO APPEAR IN!
4

PREPARE YOURSELVES FOR A REAL TREAT!
AT LONG LAST! THE FOOD!

CHUCK IS GOING TO DRAW A SKETCH OF EACH OF YOU!
SHE'S KIDDING... I HOPE!

GUYS, I'LL SHOW YOU THE SKETCHES WHEN I'VE FINISHED!

SEE?!

WOW! ROUGHEST BUNCH OF ART CRITICS I'VE EVER RUN INTO!!
...AND NOW, DOGGIES--FOR YOUR GOURMET PARTY FOOD!!
RIIIP
GRRRR
5

THE PORTIONS ARE SO SMALL!
THANK GOODNESS THEY ARE SMALL!
THIS STUFF IS REAL YUCKY!
I WOULDN'T FEED IT TO A CAT!

I REALLY APPRECIATE YOU HELPING OUT, SMITHERS!
IF YOU REALLY APPRECIATE IT, MISS VERONICA...

...YOU'LL GET SOMEONE ELSE TO DO IT NEXT YEAR!

DOESN'T IT JUST GIVE YOU ALL A NICE, WARM, FUZZY FEELING TO KNOW WE'VE SHOWN OUR FOUR-LEGGED FRIENDS HOW MUCH WE APPRECIATE THEM?

WONDER WHAT WE DID TO DESERVE THIS TREATMENT!
PROBABLY SOMETHING REAL BAD!
I HEAR SOME CRUEL MISTRESSES REPEAT THIS TORTURE YEAR... AFTER YEAR...
...NO MATTER HOW WELL YOU BEHAVE!
END

When Mrs. Lodge realizes most of Veronica's friends are having a tough time financially, she encourages Veronica to throw a "gifts from the heart" holiday party. It's one party that's priceless!

TA TA!
TA TA TO YOU, TOO!
sigh
sigh
I RECOGNIZE YOUR SIGH!
IT'S THE SIGH OF A BROKE PERSON!
YOU GOT IT!
I CAN'T AFFORD ANYTHING THIS YEAR!

I GUESS WE'LL FIGURE SOMETHING OUT!
WE ALWAYS DO!
SO...
THANKS FOR HELPING ME FOOD SHOP, MOM. I COULDN'T DO THIS BY MYSELF!
SALE

I SEE YOU'RE SHOPPING UP A STORM, RONNIE!
HI, ETHEL!
2 for 99¢
CAN SALE
DP's
JA's

I DIDN'T KNOW YOU WORKED HERE!
I HAVE TO IF I WANT SPENDING MONEY!

NOW I CAN AFFORD TO COME TO YOUR PARTY AND GET YOU A GIFT!
2 for 99¢
UH... GEE... UH...
ETHEL! DIDN'T VERONICA TELL YOU ABOUT THE NEW THEME OF HER PARTY?

THERE ARE NO STORE BOUGHT GIFTS ALLOWED!
!

REALLY?
YEAH, MOM... REALLY?

THAT'S RIGHT! ONLY GIFTS FROM THE HEART! FOR EXAMPLE, FREE TUTORING FOR A CLASS!
OR A HAND-WRITTEN POEM!
WOW!
THAT'S A RELIEF!
4

WHY DON'T WE MAKE IT A POT LUCK DINNER!
WE CAN EACH BRING A DISH!

THAT WAY YOU DON'T HAVE TO BUY ALL THIS STUFF!
IT'LL MAKE IT MUCH MORE PERSONAL!

THAT'S A GREAT IDEA ETHEL!
WHAT? Huh?

SO...
VERONICA! A STRIPPED DOWN HOLIDAY PARTY! WHAT A GREAT IDEA!
MY WALLET THANKS YOU!

THANK MY MOTHER!
AND ETHEL!
I DON'T GET THIS!
I UNDERSTAND EVERYONE IS BROKE! BUT I DON'T MIND SHARING MY WEALTH!
5

THE DAY OF THE PARTY...

HI, GUYS! WOW! THOSE SMELL GREAT!

I'LL TAKE THESE INTO THE KITCHEN AND KEEP THEM WARM!

WOW! LOOK AT ALL THAT!

6

LET'S EXCHANGE GIFTS BEFORE DINNER!
OH, GOOD!
THIS IS FROM BETTY!
"A WEEK OF ARCHIE ALL TO MYSELF!" GIFT CERTIFICATE!
WELL, ENJOY THIS...
BECAUSE I'M GIVING YOU THE SAME THING!
I'M GIVING BOTH OF YOU DIGITAL PICTURES OF US TAKEN LAST SUMMER!
I MADE THESE FRAMES MYSELF!
BEAUTIFUL!
I HAVE PICTURES FOR EVERYONE, TOO!
7

IT'S A PROFESSIONAL SHOT OF ME! FOR ALL OF YOU TO ENJOY!
WOW... LUCKY US...
THIS IS FOR YOU, JUGHEAD!
A COUPON FOR A FIVE COURSE HOME-COOKED MEAL!
YUM!
AND I HAVE A SPECIAL GIFT FOR YOU!
I ACCEPT YOUR INVITATION!
YAY!
WOW! FREE MAKEOVERS FROM GINGER!
AND GUITAR LESSONS FROM FRANKIE!
8

AND HERE'S A CD I MADE FOR EVERYONE WITH HOLIDAY SONGS ON IT.!
THANKS, BRIGITTE!
CHUCK DREW A COMIC STRIP WITH ALL OF US IN IT.!
COPIES FOR EVERYONE!

NOW THIS IS WHAT CHRISTMAS IS ALL ABOUT!
I THINK I GET IT NOW, MOM!
WE'VE GOT SOME TIME BEFORE DINNER.!

LET'S SET UP THE MP3 PLAYER!
LET'S DANCE!!
9

LOOKS LIKE THEY'RE HAVING A GOOD TIME!
I'M HAVING ONE TOO!
I'M HAPPY THINKING ABOUT ALL THE MONEY I DIDN'T SPEND ON THIS PARTY!
SOON...
DINNER TIME!
GOOD! I'M STARVED!
WOW! LOOK AT THAT SPREAD!
10

BETTY, THIS LASAGNA IS TOO MUCH!
THANKS! I LEARNED IT FROM THE RACHAEL ROY SHOW!

AND THIS HAM IS DELICIOUS!
I BROUGHT THAT!

HOW APPROPRIATE! HAM FROM THE HAM!
HARR DEE HARR HAR!

ARE YOU ENJOYING MY HOME BAKED ROLLS?
MMNFF!*
*TRANSLATION: "YOU BET!"

SO...
THAT WAS AN AWESOME DINNER!
WELL, I HOPE YOU SAVED ROOM...
BECAUSE I MADE DESSERT WITH MY OWN HANDS!
AND THAT ENDS OUR FESTIVE MEAL!
11

WOW! LOOK AT THAT CAKE! IT LOOKS AMAZING!
REMEMBER WHO MADE IT!
JUGHEAD! YOU CAN HAVE THE FIRST PIECE!
OKAY--BUT CLEAR A PATH TO THE BATHROOM FOR ME!
HOW IS IT?
IT'S DELICIOUS! OMIGOSH! VERONICA MADE A DELICIOUS DESSERT!
IT'S A CHRISTMAS MIRACLE!!
PHFAAT
I WAS GOING TO ASK FOR ANOTHER PIECE ANYWAY!
HAHA HAHA
HAPPY HOLIDAYS TO EVERY-ONE FROM ARCHIE & FRIENDS!
END

Veronica's personal chef has baked some delectably delicious pastries for the orphanage's Christmas party... but hungry Jughead has accidentally eaten them all! Can this story still end on a sweet note?

Betty and Veronica® in The PARTY

OH, GASTON! YOU'VE COMPLETELY OUTDONE YOURSELF!!

THE CHILDREN AT TONIGHT'S ORPHANAGE PARTY WILL GO BONKERS FOR YOUR PASTRIES!

FOR SURE! FOR SURE!

Script: GEORGE GLADIR | Pencils: JEFF SHULTZ | Inks: JON D'AGOSTINO | Letters: JACK MORELLI | Colors: BARRY GROSSMAN

WHAT'S UP, JUGGIE?
I'VE BEEN RINGING THIS BELL ALL DAY FOR A LOCAL CHARITY! ...AND BOY, AM I BUSHED!

IF YOU DON'T MIND WAITING WHILE WE RUN A FEW ERRANDS, WE'LL GIVE YOU A LIFT HOME!
HEY! THAT'D BE GREAT!

I JUST HAVE TO DROP OFF THE MONEY I COLLECTED! I'LL BE RIGHT BACK!

HE LOOKS FAMISHED! MAYBE WE CAN GIVE HIM ONE OF THE PASTRIES?
I SHOULD SAY NOT!! WE BARELY HAVE ENOUGH FOR THE ORPHANS!

HERE HE COMES!
Oh, MAN! I COULD FALL ASLEEP ON THIS COLD SIDEWALK RIGHT NOW!

LIE DOWN IN HERE WHILE BETTY AND I GO PICK UP SOME PARTY FAVORS!
2

yawn!
WHERE AM I?

WHAT IS THAT DELICIOUS SMELL?
SNIFF
SNIFF

MAN! I MUST BE IN HOG HEAVEN!

I'VE NEVER GOBBLE! GOBBLE! TASTED ANYTHING GOBBLE! CHOMP! SO GOOD!

Whew! THAT SURE HIT THE SPOT!
NOW I CAN GO BACK TO SLEEP IN COMFORT!

LOOKS LIKE JUGHEAD IS STILL ASLEEP!
3

HE'S ONLY PRETENDING TO BE ASLEEP!
LOOK! HE'S DEVOURED ALL THE PASTRIES!!
LODGE

HOW COULD YOU BE SUCH A PIG?!
Huh?
YOU'VE DEPRIVED THE POOR ORPHANS OF ALL THOSE GOODIES WE WERE BRINGING TO THEM!

OUT! YOU SCOUNDREL! YOU CAN WALK HOME FOR ALL WE CARE!
B-BUT, BUT...

HOW WAS I SUPPOSED TO KNOW?
Oh, THOSE POOR ORPHANS!

THERE HAS TO BE SOME WAY I CAN REDEEM MYSELF!

AND... THERE IS!!
SNAP

ARCHIE!! YESTERDAY YOU ASKED ME IF I'D HELP YOU SHOVEL WALKWAYS TODAY!
YEAH, BUT I WAS ONLY KIDDING! I FIGURED YOU WOULDN'T REALLY BE INTERESTED!

WELL, I AM!
I NEED MONEY DESPERATELY!
THEN GRAB A SHOVEL! WE'VE GOT A WHOLE LIST OF PLACES TO CLEAN!

SHOOF
SHOOF
SHOOF
MAN! LOOK AT THAT WHIRLING DERVISH GO!
I WONDER WHY HE NEEDS MONEY SO BADLY?

LATER...
WELL, HERE'S YOUR SHARE OF THE MONEY WE MADE!
THANKS!

I JUST HOPE I'M NOT TOO LATE!
BAKERS

AT THE RIVERDALE ORPHANAGE...
CHUCK, WE'RE SO GLAD YOU VOLUNTEERED TO DO CARICATURES OF THE KIDS!
YESTERDAY, THEY WERE ALL SO VERY DISAPPOINTED WHEN BETTY AND I SHOWED UP WITHOUT THE PROMISED PASTRIES!
THAT THIEVING HOG JUGHEAD ATE THEM ALL UP ON US!
YEAH!

WELL, THE THIEVIN' HOG IS HERE TO MAKE AMENDS!
?

HERE YOU ARE, GUYS'N'GALS-- HELP YOUR-SELVES!

JUGHEAD! I CAN'T BELIEVE YOU'RE DOING THIS!
THAT MAKES TWO OF US!
I CAN'T BELIEVE IT EITHER!
Merry CHRISTMAS
END

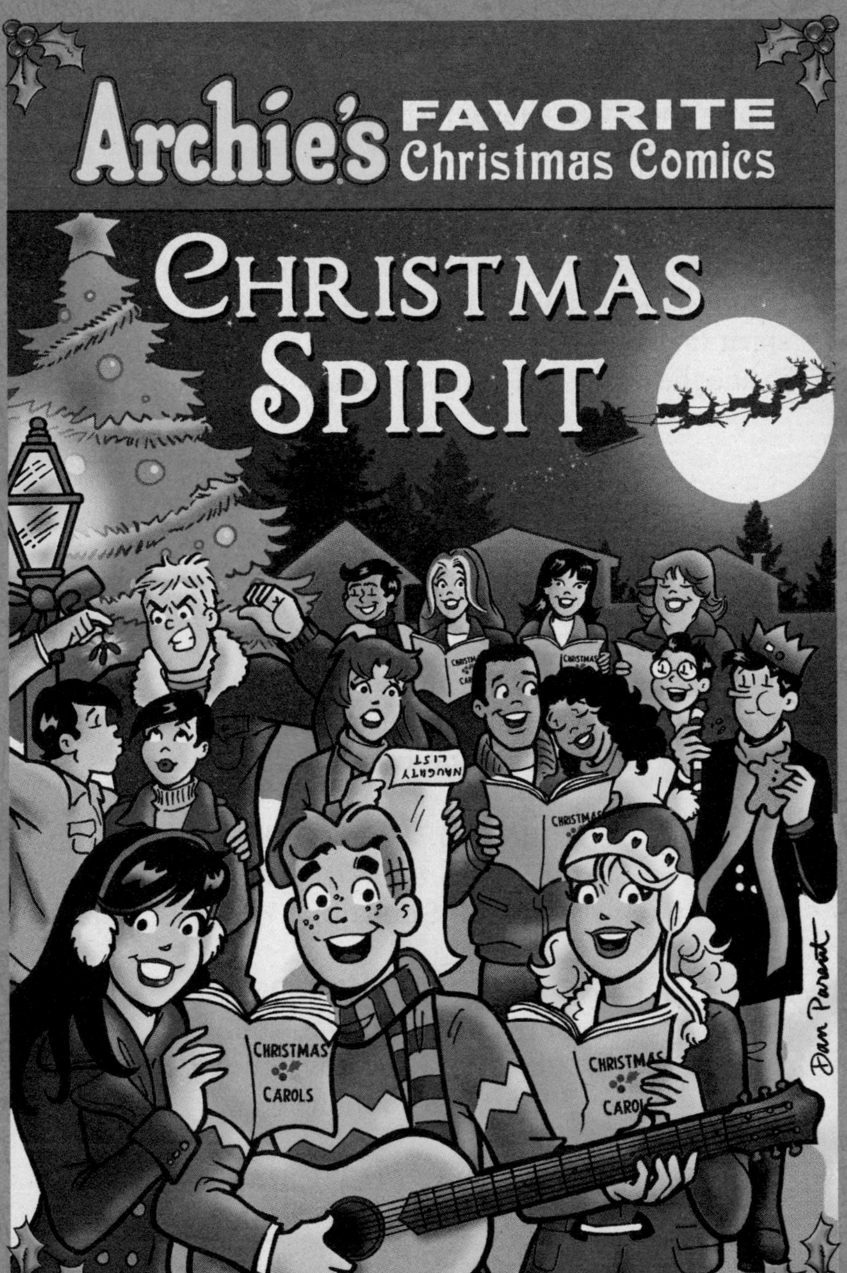
Archie's FAVORITE Christmas Comics
CHRISTMAS SPIRIT
NAUGHTY LIST
CHRISTMAS CAROLS
CHRISTMAS CAROLS
Dan Parent

If ever there was a town just oozing with Christmas spirit, it's Riverdale, USA! From festive decorations to delightful festivals and everything in-between, Archie's fabled home town pulls out all the stops for the holidays. Of course, the town's teens are "all-in" when it comes to holiday cheer, and these stories reflect that spirit that shines both on the town's exterior as well as inside the hearts of Riverdale's residents.

YOU'RE COOKED
Veronica #176, 2007
by Dan Parent, Jim Amash,
Barry Grossman and Teresa Davidson

SHE NEEDS A LITTLE CHRISTMAS
***Betty & Veronica #132*, 1999**
by Kathleen Webb, Dan DeCarlo, Henry Scarpelli,
Barry Grossman and Bill Yoshida

A COUPLE OF FRUITCAKES
***Betty & Veronica #169*, 2002**
by Kathleen Webb, Jeff Shultz and Henry Scarpelli

HERE WE COME A-CAROLING
Holiday Fun Digest #8, 2003
by Greg Crosby, Tim Kennedy, Rudy Lapick
and Bill Yoshida

ARCHIE'S HOLIDAY FUN SCRAPBOOK
***Holiday Fun Digest #12*, 2007**
by Dan Parent

A Christmas tree was never sweeter when Betty and Veronica decide to bake this year's ornaments... but can they keep Jughead from undecorating the tree?!

Veronica YOU'RE COOKED!

VERONICA! WHAT'S ALL THIS?

I'VE BEEN BITTEN BY THE HOLIDAY COOKING BUG!

Uh-- YOU-- WELL...
NO OFFENSE, DEAR, BUT YOU KNOW HOW YOU ARE IN THE KITCHEN!

AND THAT'S WHY I'M HERE!
BETTY! THANK GOODNESS!

GO TO IT, GIRLS!

SOON...
Mmmm... THOSE COOKIES LOOK DELICIOUS!
HANDS OFF! THEY'RE FOR THE TREE!

AND SOON...
WE'VE GOT THE POPCORN STRING AND CANDY CANES UP!
TIME FOR THE GINGERBREAD MEN!
2

SOON...
WOW! BEAUTIFUL!
GREAT JOB, GIRLS!

LET'S GET BACK INTO THE KITCHEN!
YOU'RE DOING MORE?!

YES! WE'RE GOING TO MAKE A GINGERBREAD VILLAGE!
WELL, DON'T LET ME STAND IN YOUR WAY!

SO...
WOW! THESE DIRECTIONS ARE COMPLICATED!
WE'VE GOT ALL THESE LITTLE BUILDINGS DONE!
THE TOWN HALL IS THE REAL CHALLENGE!
3

LATER...
GIRLS, IT'S LATE! AND YOU BOTH LOOK EXHAUSTED!
WHY DON'T YOU STAY OVERNIGHT, BETTY?

YOU GIRLS CAN FINISH UP IN THE MORNING.
GOOD IDEA!

EARLY NEXT MORNING...
YOU GIRLS ARE AT IT SO EARLY!
JUST FINISHING UP.

THE VILLAGE IS BEAUTIFUL!
ALL THE BUILDINGS ARE MADE OF GINGERBREAD...

...WITH A BASE MADE OF FRUITCAKE!
YOU GIRLS HAVE OUTDONE YOURSELVES!

YOU'VE WORKED HARD...
GET DRESSED AND I'LL TAKE YOU OUT FOR BRUNCH!
4

LATER...
THAT BRUNCH WAS DELICIOUS! THANK YOU, MRS. LODGE!
MY PLEASURE, BETTY!
GAK!
OUR VILLAGE ...CRUMBS!!!
AND THE TREE'S BEEN EATEN BARE!!!
EVEN THE FRUITCAKE BASE IS GONE! WHO LIKES FRUITCAKE?!

SORRY, GIRLS! I TRIED TO STOP HIM!
WE CAME OVER TO HANG OUT!

WHILE I WAS IN THE BATHROOM, HE WENT CRAZY!
Uh-oh... OKAY, LET ME HAVE IT.

Aw, IT'S CHRISTMAS! I CAN'T GET MAD. DID YOU AT LEAST ENJOY IT?
IT WAS SCRUMPTIOUS!
WELL, I KNOW WHAT WE CAN DO TODAY...
...LET'S REBUILD THAT VILLAGE!
HERE, JUGHEAD, MIX THIS. AND DON'T EAT IT!
THIS IS FUN!
GASTON, I THINK YOU'VE GOT TODAY OFF!
END

Betty is having a "blue Christmas"—she just can't compete with Veronica when it comes to buying Christmas gifts. Will Veronica come through with the gift of friendship?

HI, BETTY! WHEW! WHAT A HAUL, HUH? AND I STILL GOT TONS MORE SHOPPING LEFT TO DO!

ISN'T CHRISTMAS WONDERFUL?

(GULP) WELL, IT WAS JUST A FEW MINUTES AGO!

Le Shop

MEGA MALL

PLAZA

RIVERDALE MALL

Betty and Veronica in

"She Needs A Little Christmas"

MERRY CHRISTMAS, BETTY!
`LO, JUGGIE! (SNIFF)

WHAT'S THE MATTER? WHY AREN'T YOU FULL OF YOUR USUAL CHRISTMAS CHEER?
OH, IT'S NOTHING, REALLY...!

RON'S BUYING POWER MAKES MY ATTEMPTS AT GIFT-GIVING LOOK PUNY, PALTRY AND PATHETIC!
NICE ALLITERATION!

(SIGH) I'D BUY THE MOON AND STARS FOR FRIENDS AND FAMILY IF I HAD AS MUCH MONEY AS SHE DOES!

(SIGH) ALL THE JOY'S GONE RIGHT OUT OF MY CHRISTMAS!

MERRY CHRISTMAS, JUGHEAD!
BAH! HUMBUG TO YOU, EBENEEZER SCROOGE!
SHOP
2

WHAT'S WITH WAVING ALL YOUR WEALTH AT BETTY?
OOOH, NICE ALLITERATION!
SHOP
MALL

WHAT ARE YOU TALKING ABOUT? ALL I DID WAS WALK PAST HER CARRYING MY PACKAGES!

SHE'S BLUE BECAUSE YOU OUTSPENT HER IN GIFT SHOPPING!
SO, WHAT'S NEW? I DO THAT EVERY YEAR!

YEAH, BUT THIS YEAR SHE THOUGHT SHE'D BOUGHT THE PERFECT GIFTS FOR EVERYONE!
YOUR HAUL MADE HER EFFORTS SEEM INADEQUATE!

SHE SAYS HER CHRISTMAS SPIRIT IS ALL GONE!
AND SHE'S THE ONE WHO KEEPS TELLING ME THAT CHRISTMAS IS MORE THAN PRESENTS!
SPECIAL

MAYBE IT'S YOUR TURN TO REMIND HER!
YOU KNOW, JUGGIE, YOU'RE RIGHT... AND I KNOW JUST WHERE TO START!
3

LATER...
BING! BONG!
IT'S AFTER SUPPER ON A SCHOOL NIGHT! WHO COULD THAT BE ?

MERRY CHRISTMAS, BETTY! GET YOUR COLD WEATHER GEAR ON! YOU'RE COMING WITH ME!
HUH?

(GASP) A HORSE AND SLEIGH ?
YEP! HOP IN!

I PACKED A THERMOS OF HOT CHOCOLATE AND SOME CHRISTMAS COOKIES!
WE'RE GOING TO GO LOOK AT THE LIGHTS ON NOVELTY HILL ROAD!

OH, WOW, RON, THIS IS BEAUTIFUL! AND LOOK! THE MOON IS RISING OVER THE HILL!
LOOK AT THOSE FIELDS COVERED WITH SNOW AND GLEAMING IN THE MOONLIGHT!
4

CHERRY VALLEY CHURCH IS ALL LIT UP!
ISN'T IT BEAUTIFUL?

LISTEN! YOU CAN HEAR THEIR CAROLLERS SINGING!
LET'S JOIN IN!

JINGLE BELLS... JINGLE BELLS...

OH, RON, THIS HAS BEEN ABSOLUTELY WONDERFUL! YOU'VE GIVEN ME BACK THE MAGIC TO MY CHRISTMAS!
I KNEW I COULD!

YOU'RE THE ONE WHO ALWAYS SAYS THERE SHOULD BE MORE GIVING THAN GETTING ON CHRISTMAS!
BESIDES... BETWEEN YOU AND ME...

... ALL THE STUFF I BOUGHT EARLIER WAS JUST FOR ME!
I SHOULD HAVE KNOWN! MERRY CHRISTMAS, VERONICA!
End

Veronica gets a bad taste in her mouth when she learns whose relative is actually responsible for the Lodge family fruitcake recipe!

Betty and Veronica in "A Couple of Fruitcakes"

I USUALLY DON'T LIKE FRUITCAKE, VERONICA, BUT THE ONE GASTON BAKES FOR YOUR FAMILY IS DELICIOUS!

IT IS GOOD, ISN'T IT?

IT WOULD BE A WASTE OF YOUR TIME!
WHAT? YOU DON'T THINK I COULD BAKE ONE AS GOOD AS HIS?

YOU WOULDN'T HAVE A CHANCE TO TRY! AS I SAID, IT'S BEEN IN OUR FAMILY FOR GENERATIONS...

...AND IT'S GOING TO STAY THAT WAY! GASTON HAS ORDERS NOT TO GIVE THE RECIPE TO ANYONE!

EVEN YOU!
WHAT? AFRAID I'LL MAKE A BETTER ONE?

DON'T YOU HAVE ANY SECRET FAMILY RECIPES?
WELL, THERE'S GRANNY COOPER'S RECIPE FOR PICKLED PERSIMMON PRESERVES...

...BUT SINCE MY WHOLE FAMILY AGREES IT OUGHT TO STAY A SECRET, I DON'T THINK IT QUALIFIES!
VERY FUNNY!
2

I'LL LET YOU TAKE SOME FRUITCAKE HOME TO SHARE WITH YOUR FAMILY, BUT THAT'S THE BEST I CAN DO!

THE RECIPE FOR THE FAMOUS LODGE GUILDED FRUITCAKE MUST REMAIN A HEAVILY GUARDED SECRET!
SHUCKS!

IT'S NOT LIKE I WAS GONNA SELL IT ON THE OPEN MARKET!
SELL WHAT? LODGE FAMILY SECRETS?

YOU'RE CLOSE, JUG! RON WON'T GIVE ME THE RECIPE FOR HER FAMOUS FRUITCAKE THAT YOU'RE EATING!
HECK! IS THAT ALL?

I'LL GIVE YOU THE RECIPE! IT'S THE SAME AS MY MOM'S!
IMPOSSIBLE! IT'S STAYED IN MY FAMILY FOR YEARS!

MAYBE IT WANDERED OUT ONCE!
NOT LIKELY!
THERE'S A WAY TO FIND OUT! SHOW JUGGIE'S RECIPE TO GASTON!
3

FORTUNATELY, I'VE HELPED MY MOM BAKE IT SO OFTEN, I'VE GOT IT MEMORIZED!
PROBABLY BECAUSE HE EATS IT AS FAST AS SHE BAKES IT!

ZUT ALORS!! WHERE DID YOU GET ZIS RECIPE?
IT'S BEEN IN MY FAMILY FOR YEARS!

IT WAS HANDED DOWN BY MY GREAT-GREAT UNCLE MALACHI! HE WAS A COOK!
MALACHI JONES?
RECIPES

LOOK AT ZE BOTTOM OF ZE RECIPE CARD FOR ZE LODGE GUILDED FRUITCAKE!
IT'S SIGNED MALACHI JONES!

HE MUST'VE BEEN A COOK FOR THE LODGE FAMILY AT ONE TIME!
YOU... YOU MEAN HE INTRODUCED THE FAMOUS LODGE GUILDED FRUITCAKE INTO OUR HOLIDAY MENU?!?

UH-HUH! BUT IT'S ACTUALLY CALLED "POOR MAN'S FRUITCAKE"!
PEOPLE USED TO MAKE IT WHEN THEY COULDN'T AFFORD INGREDIENTS FOR A FANCY FRUIT-CAKE!
4

GASTON!! YOU MEAN TO TELL ME WE'VE BEEN CONSUMING A CHEAP VERSION OF FRUITCAKE ALL THESE YEARS?!

CHEAP?! GASTON DOES NOT MAKE ZE CHEAP FRUITCAKE! NOT WIZ MARZIPAN ICING, GILDED WIZ EDIBLE GOLD!
SO THAT'S HOW YOU'VE BEEN FANCYING IT UP FOR THE LODGES!

YOU CAN DRESS IT UP ALL YOU LIKE, BUT THAT DOESN'T CHANGE THE FACT THAT IT'S MADE FOR FAR MORE INFERIOR TASTES!
YOU'VE BEEN HAPPILY SNARFING IT DOWN FOR YEARS!

WHAT ARE YOU BELLOWING ABOUT NOW, VERONICA?
YOUR DAUGHTER'S BECOMING SNOBBISH OVER A FRUITCAKE!

GOOD! I'VE WANTED HER TO STOP DATING THAT IMBECILE ARCHIE ANDREWS FOR YEARS!

ANYBODY GOT A LOADED FRUITCAKE I CAN DROP ON MY TOE?
HOW ABOUT A SLICE OF HUMBLE PIE INSTEAD?
End

From a duo to a trio to a full-fledged glee club, Archie and his friends work their Christmas magic and turn a caroling crew into an entire chorus!

Archie in "HERE WE COME A-CAROLING"

SCRIPT: GREG CROSBY
PENCILS: TIM KENNEDY
INKS: RUDY LAPICK
LETTERS: BILL YOSHIDA

JINGLE BELLS... JINGLE ALL THE WAY...

CHIPPO'S

SODA

COME ON, ARCHIE... JOIN US!
WE'VE GOT EXTRA SONG BOOKS WITH US!

OKAY- PROMISE TO KEEP ME WARM IF I GET COLD?

WE'LL SANDWICH YOU IN BETWEEN US LIKE A COOKIE!
FANTASTIC!

OH, DASHING THROUGH THE SNOW... IN A ONE-HORSE OPEN SLEIGH...

HI! WHAT'S GOING ON?
HELLO, MOOSE! WE'RE GOING THROUGH THE NEIGHBORHOOD SING-ING CHRISTMAS CAROLS! WANT TO JOIN US?

DUH... I CAN'T SING TOO GOOD, BUT IT LOOKS LIKE FUN!
GRAB A SONG BOOK!
2

UP ON THE ROOF TOP REINDEERS PAUSE... OUT JUMPS GOOD OLD SANTA CLAUS...

MIDGE- COME ON AND JOIN US!
OH, GOODY!

WHERE ARE WE GOING?
JUST WALKING THROUGH THE NEIGHBORHOOD, GOING TO ALL OUR FRIENDS' HOUSES AND CAROLLING!

DECK THE HALLS WITH
BOUGHS OF HOLLY...

FA LA LA LA LA- LA LA LA LA...
HI, REGGIE!
3

YOU GUYS ARE HAVING ALL THE FUN, MIND IF I JUMP IN, TOO?
THE MORE THE MERRIER!

MIND IF I SHARE YOUR SONG BOOK, TOOTS?
HERE'S ONE OF YOUR OWN!

JINGLE BELLS, JINGLE BELLS, JINGLE ALL THE WAY...

OH, WHAT FUN IT IS TO RIDE IN A ONE...
SODA

JUGHEAD! COME ALONG AND JOIN US!
BE RIGHT OUT!
4

MAY I COME ALONG?
SURE!
HEY, I WANT TO SING, TOO!
WAIT FOR ME!

HEY, I JUST THOUGHT OF SOMETHING! EVERYBODY WE KNOW HAS JOINED US! LOOK... EVERYONE'S HERE!

THERE'S NO ONE LEFT TO SING CAROLS TO!
OH, YES THERE IS!
SNAP!

'TIS THE SEASON TO BE JOLLY, FA, LA, LA, LA, LA, LA, LA, LA, LA, LA...
END

The holidays are the perfect time to relive cherished holiday memories! As you pore through Archie and his friends' festive "scrapbook" you'll witness many merry milestones, including Archie's discovery of mistletoe, Betty and Veronica's first gift-shopping sprees, Jughead's first holiday buffet and Reggie's first mirror!

AW, WASN'T I A CUTE BABY?
AW, I'M A CUTIE TOO!
I WAS ELEGANT... EVEN THEN!
I THINK WE WERE ALL PRETTY CUTE!
...ESPECIALLY ME!
2

I REMEMBER WHEN SANTA BROUGHT ME MY FIRST DOLLY!
AND I REMEMBER MY FIRST SUB SANDWICH...IT WAS TURKEY AND CHEESE!
I REMEMBER MY FIRST TIARA! I WAS MAD THAT IT HAD ONLY ONE DIAMOND IN IT!
AH, MY FIRST MIRROR! WHAT A BEAUTIFUL SIGHT TO BEHOLD!
3

THIS WAS MY FIRST VISIT TO SANTA AT THE RIVERDALE MALL!
I ASKED FOR, AND GOT, MY FIRST TRAIN SET!
I NEVER GOT A TURN! VERONICA TIED UP ALL SANTA'S TIME WITH HER 13 PAGE CHRISTMAS LIST!
REMEMBER WHEN I GOT MY FIRST E-Z COOK OVEN? I MADE ARCHIE THE FIRST OF MANY DELICIOUS CAKES FOR YEARS TO COME!
E-Z
AND WHEN VERONICA GOT HER FIRST E-Z COOK OVEN, IT WAS THE MEMORY OF MY FIRST BARF!!
4

REMEMBER IN KINDERGARTEN WHEN WE DISCOVERED MISTLETOE?
YES, I DO!
AND HOW ABOUT THAT BEAUTIFUL GINGERBREAD HOUSE WE MADE?
YES, IT WAS BEAUTIFUL FOR THE FIVE MINUTES IT LASTED!
5

OH LOOK! IT WAS OUR FIRST YEAR CHRISTMAS CAROLING!
WHY ARE ALL THOSE DOGS THERE?
VERONICA'S VOICE ATTRACTED DOGS FROM ALL OVER RIVERDALE!
LOOK! TWO-TIMING ARCHIE WAS ALREADY AT IT AT AGE 8!
THAT REALLY HELPED PERFECT OUR AIM, DIDN'T IT BETTY?
6

LOOK AT THIS COOL SNOWMAN WE MADE!
IT DOESN'T COMPARE TO MY FIRST MASTERPIECE!
REMEMBER OUR FIRST CHRISTMAS DANCE IN JUNIOR HIGH?
NOBODY COULD TWO-TIME US IN SUCH HOLIDAY FASHION AS ARCHIE!
ADMIT ONE
Riverdale Junior High Christmas Dance
7

THIS IS MY FIRST CHRISTMAS WITH MY NEW SISTER JELLYBEAN!
Baby's 1st Christmas
MERRY Christmas BEtty from ARCHIE
HERE'S THE FIRST CHRISTMAS CARD YOU MADE FOR ME ARCHIE! THIS CARD WAS ALWAYS PRECIOUS TO ME!
Too VERonica MERRY Christmas from ARCHIE
WOW! I JUST FIGURED YOU WERE TOO CHEAP TO BUY A CHRISTMAS GIFT!
POP'S
POP TATE TO THE RESCUE ON A COLD DAY!
8

I REMEMBER THE YEAR I SAW SANTA OUTSIDE AND TRIED TO SNAP A *PICTURE!* IT DIDN'T COME OUT VERY WELL...
Betty
I SNAPPED THIS SHOT OF SANTA ONE YEAR! HE SAID IT WAS OKAY SINCE I WAS SUCH A *GOOD GIRL!*
I LEARNED THE HARD WAY SANTA DOESN'T LIKE HIS PICTURE TAKEN!
BUT SANTA ALWAYS SEEMS TO COME THROUGH-- WHETHER WE'RE *NAUGHTY* OR *NICE!*
9

THERE'S NOTHING LIKE ALL THE CAREFREE *HOLIDAY FUN* WE'VE HAD!
PLAYING OUTSIDE ALL DAY IN THE SNOW!
I HAVE SO MANY FOND MEMORIES OF HOLIDAY *SHOPPING!*
Sale
I GET EMOTIONAL WHEN I THINK OF SOME OF THOSE GREAT HOLIDAY *BUFFETS!*
10

IT'S WEIRD HOW EVERYBODY SEEMS SO NICE THIS TIME OF YEAR!
YOU WANT TO BE FRIENDLY TO EVERYONE YOU SEE!
WELL, ALMOST EVERYONE!
BUT IT MAKES YOU REALIZE HOW LUCKY WE ALL ARE!
HAVING THE FAMILIES AND FRIENDS WE HAVE MAKE OUR HOLIDAYS SO GREAT!
11

ONE THING IS FOR SURE! THERE'S NO PLACE LIKE RIVERDALE AT CHRISTMAS TIME!
POP'S
POP'S
Happy Holidays
FROM ARCHIE & THE GANG!
END